TARGET: The Lincoln Tunnel. A three-mile, two-lane corridor running beneath the Hudson River. Booby traps covered every inch of it. Th[illegible]oln Tunnel was a gauntlet of death.

DESTINATION: Nuked [illegible]viet megatons worth of the most [illegible]ation in the history of human [illegible]d for Contams, zombie scavs, [illegible]s hand-picked paramilitary el[illegible]nmando Retaliatory Force, SCC[illegible]

STRATEGY: To d[illegible] automatic-weapons fire, armo[illegible]riers of high-tensile steel netting [illegible]g obstacles in a suicide scramble thr[illegible] in a kill-or-be-killed dead man's run thr[illegible]aviest firepower SCORF can muster.

WHEELMAN: Magnus Trench, a.k.a. Phoenix.

Also in the PHOENIX series:

 # 1: DARK MESSIAH
 # 2: GROUND ZERO
 # 3: DEATH QUEST
 # 4: METALSTORM

Alas!
Lonely sits the city,
Once great with people!
She that was great among nations,
Is become like a widow.
—*Lamentations, I:1*

For they have sown the wind,
And they shall reap the whirlwind.
—*Hosea, VIII:7*

Prologue

Once upon a time, there was a place called hell.

On earth.

The name of that hell was Nuked York City.

And somewhere in that hell, in a hotzone called Coney Island, by a toxic ocean where fish no longer swam, under the blistering rays of a sun no longer tamed by a shield of ozone in the stratosphere—a sun which glowed a fiery red as its dying rays slanted in smoky shafts across heaps of slag that had once been rows of middle-class homes—zombie scavengers scuttled like human maggots across a field of garbage, all silently making for a single wreckage zone as night descended and the packs of feral dogs which lurked on the fringes of the place began to howl for meat and blood.

As night crashed to the broken rubble, they would continue to gather on their sacred place from miles around.

Strange and great things would happen in the darkness tonight. In the vast basement of one of the concrete towers of the derelict city housing projects, the warlord's squeeze was giving birth.

She had shown the signs for days, and by this day's noon had experienced the first contractions. The Tellers had decreed that the squeeze would produce no ordinary child.

The squeeze had come to term in only three months. Her hair and teeth had fallen out and the fat and muscle tissue of her body and limbs had quickly shrunk to almost nothing.

All the while her womb developed to an abnormal size so that it was impossible for her to walk and she had to be carried about wherever she went.

Bizarre dreams had also come to the squeeze. Visions of a colossus which bestrode the earth, breathing fire and eating men as though they were insects, tormented her. The visions continued even while she was awake.

When they possessed her, she would fall to the ground, convulsing and speaking in tongues, voiding her bowels and her bladder while blood oozed through the pores of her skin.

The people of the tribe whispered of putting her to death, but did no more than whisper. Although they were mortally afraid that the squeeze would bring a terrible thing into the world, a hell child that could consume them all, they knew that to voice any opposition would mean being impaled on a telephone pole with icepicks and left to the dog packs in the night.

Abraxas, their warlord, had decreed that the child should live.

Abraxas, who called himself the Wizard of Oz.

An iron mask covered the warlord's face. The face behind the mask was itself a mask. The intense heat of nuclear detonations had flashburned the flesh to a hideous mass of scar tissue.

The mind beneath the scar tissue was even uglier. The soul worse.

Abraxas didn't care.

Abraxas was the light and the power. His was the glory. His was the strength that unified the tribes of Oz. His was the might which decreed that "here goes life" or "there goes death." Only Abraxas knew or cared which direction the life or death he decreed took.

Torches lit the woman at the feet of Abraxas as the squeeze lay naked on a filthy mattress on the moist concrete floor of the housing project tower's basement.

She lay in the agony of childbirth. It had not gone well with her. Her womb was huge, distended. She lay moaning and writhing on the cold stone floor. Her moment was near.

"Noooooooooo!"

The woman's shriek reverberated across the cold stone cavern of the abandoned housing project's cavernous basement, causing the faces at the perimeter of fire to withdraw in fear.

"Kill meeeeee!"

Abraxas nodded. Two men firmly grasped the woman's wrists as she thrashed in agonized convulsions. A third man stood behind her head, the muzzle of a pump-action shotgun pointed an inch from the back of her head.

Again Abraxas nodded.

The old woman stepped forward, rags covering her body, gently opening the thrashing woman's legs.

The convulsions became stronger. The birthing woman's eyes rolled up in her face and her body arched in a spasm of utter agony. Now something strange was happening.

The flesh of the womb stood out in places, as though something were prodding it from within.

Down near the navel of the abnormally large womb something round made an impression on the surface of the skin.

It was a face. Nose and mouth and eyes. Then the impressions of teeth and gums. A horrible keening wail rose up from the woman. It did not come from her mouth. It was coming from inside her womb.

Beneath the face and a little to either side, the indentation of fingers. Clawed fingers.

The howling from inside the womb got louder.

The woman's eyes suddenly widened and her lips drew back, but no sound came from her mouth. Instead, a fountain of bright blood jetted from inside her throat, running thickly between her heaving breasts.

A moment later, the thing she had been carrying inside her used its taloned hands to rip through the membrance of the womb.

Snarling, it lay across the husk of the woman who had conceived it, gathering its strength, its scales glistening on its iridescent body, its multifaceted bee eyes reflecting the mind-searing horror on the faces of the people as they watched this atrocity given birth.

Abraxas had a son.

At a nod from his warlord, the scarfaced man standing behind the woman in labor triggered a mercy blast that destroyed her head and ended her misery.

Forever.

Book One:
Sow the Wind . . .

Behold I cry out of wrong, but I am not heard:
I cry aloud, but there is no judgment.
He hath fenced up my way that I cannot pass, and he hath set darkness in my paths.
He hath stripped me of my glory, and taken the crown from my head.
He hath destroyed me on every side, and I am gone: and mine hope hath he removed like a tree.
He hath also kindled his wrath against me, and he counteth me unto him as one of his enemies.

—Job

Part I:

Life in the Blast Lane

1

Target: The Lincoln Tunnel. A three-mile, two-lane corridor running beneath the Hudson River, beginning in New Jersey and terminating on the West Side of Midtown Manhattan. Booby traps covered every inch of it. The Lincoln Tunnel was a gauntlet of death.

Destination: Nuked York City, 200 Soviet megatons worth of the most awesome urban devastation in the history of human warfare. Killing ground for Contams, zombie scavs, and the Dark Messiah's handpicked paramilitary elite, the Special Commando Retaliatory Force, SCORF.

Strategy: Dare concentrated automatic-weapons fire, armor-shredding mines, barriers and high-tensile steel netting, and other death-dealing obstacles in a suicide scramble through the hell tunnel in a kill-or-be-killed dead man's run through the heaviest firepower SCORF can muster.

Hardware: A Greyhound tour bus, specially modified with three-inch wraparound armor plating, armored tire guards, and a turbocharged engine, equipped with a General Electric M134 Minigun mounted on its roof—a weapon capable of spitting out up to six thousand rounds of 7.62-mm NATO rounds in just under 60 seconds.

Wheelman: Magnus Trench, a.k.a. Phoenix. The most wanted individual in the postnuclear purgatory of

America called CONUS, for Continental U.S. by its twisted rulers. A man who, it is said, can't be killed, though many have tried. A warrior who carries locked within his bloodstream the potent Alpha-Immune antibodies which can neutralize the Soviet mutant-causing virus called Plague.

Sidegunners: DeLaCour. A shaven-head giant with plates of stainless steel belted to his ribcage and the right half of his skull. A man liberated from the maniacal thralldom in which the biker honcho of Houston, Texas, called Runamok had held him for years. Liberated by the man called Phoenix, and owing the man who had freed him much more than just his life.

Raven. A female of the species deadlier than any male. Her usual weapon of choice, an aluminum crossbow firing explosive-tipped arrows, now put aside in favor of an M60 belt-fed light machine gun. A lady who's more than willing to hold up her end of a firefight. An ass-kicking femme fatale. Like DeLaCour, Raven owes Phoenix her life.

Time: The future.

Now.

2

Magnus Trench gripped the wheel and stared at a hell-blasted expanse through the crisscrossing metal bars which formed the windshield of the converted tour bus.

Between the armored crash vehicle and the gaping concrete hole carved into the rock face of the Palisades cliffs was a sterile zone of bulldozed earth.

The perimeter of the sterile zone was guarded with SCORF troops riding heavily armed APCs. The barrels of the .50-caliber machine guns on them were trained to incinerate any crash vehicle in a deathstorm of razoring steel.

Beyond the fortified entrance to the Lincoln Tunnel, over the Palisades and across the leaden gray Hudson River in the clear air of a cold November morning, was visible the twisted wreckage of Midtown Manhattan.

A thick brown photochemical smog, the color of shit and smelling even worse, swirled around the chewed-off stumps of the once-proud skyscrapers which had made it the single most recognizable skyline in the world.

All that was left now were the hell-scorched and blackened remains of the raped and murdered city of New York, lying dead on its island like a barbecued corpse on a morgue slab.

Phoenix smiled grimly. *Dead on Arrival,* it should be marked.

The corpse of this once-great metropolis had been a

destination he had fought a long, hard battle to come within sight of.

Inside the Nuked Apple he would finally learn the answer to the question which had been plaguing him since the awesome day of final reckoning on which the Soviet nukes blew his country into a thousand mushroom clouds of incandescent death, and tore his life into a million agonized fragments.

Inside the Manhattan hellzone Trench hoped that he would learn the fate of his wife Sandra and his son Brian.

After evading the relentless manhunt which the Dark Messiah had launched following Phoenix's crushing blow to Luther Enoch's plans for a postnuclear New Order in the smoldering ruins of San Francisco, Phoenix had finally reached his destination. New York City.

Trench and his two companions had made a run on a SCORF base in New Jersey. There they'd taken the Minigun. They'd picked up the bus that same week. For the next two weeks they had holed up in the ruins of a converted warehouse working on the mammoth tour bus and planning their gate-crashing strategy.

The refurbished Greyhound bus had been specially armored to withstand the brutal firepower which Phoenix, DeLaCour, and Raven knew they would encounter on their express run into Manhattan. But nothing short of a direct LAW rocket strike could so much as dent the three-inch-thick armor plate DeLaCour and Phoenix had riveted to the coach's frame.

Around the hole they'd cut in the roof so DeLaCour could fire the Minigun, they'd mounted a riveted steel pillbox impervious to bullets, with a 180-degree slit at the front and rear, so that the steel man could have maximum coverage with the lethal automatic weapon.

While Phoenix piloted the Greyhound war wagon, DeLaCour would kick ass with the 7.62 blitzkreig cannon. Strapped into the shotgun seat beside him,

Raven would have her hands full with a belt-fed M60 machine gun. The little lady was a past master with the big bad weapon, even though the MG was almost as large as she.

Even though they stood as much chance as a snowball on a red-hot griddle of making it alive through the punishing defensive array which SCORF had waiting in the Lincoln Tunnel, Phoenix and his crew had no other choice but to run the lethal gauntlet and pray they got lucky.

The Lincoln Tunnel was the only way into Manhattan.

Manhattan was where Magnus Trench's wife and kid had been last seen alive. But it was also one of the most heavily fortified prisons on the planet.

The SCORF presence in this Urban Containment Zone was a major one. The Dark Messiah's troops were crawling over the rubble like swarms of human insects.

And, to further raise the odds against them, Phoenix and his crew were expected. Phoenix was known to be heading for New York. Just *when* was not known, but the defenses would be on full alert and primed for a showdown.

An all-out, full-frontal assault was the only way to get their butts into the Zone, even if they were dead once the shooting stopped.

At least they had tried to give themselves the best chance possible of pulling off what they were about to attempt. They had waited until three in the morning. The night was moonless and the guards around the outer perimeter had just been changed.

It was now or never.

Phoenix threw the clutch into gear. The motor came alive with a powerful roar, like a jungle cat getting ready to pounce. DeLaCour belted himself in behind the Minigun, snapped in the belt of 7.62-mm heart-rippers, and cranked a live round into the chamber.

Raven flashed Phoenix the thumbs-up and cranked the M60's bolt action to chamber a 7.62 steel-jacket round, shoving the weapon's muzzle through one of the firing ports in the Greyhound's armored hull.

The Dark Messiah's Armageddon shock troops might be capable of destroying anything that came their way with frightening ease.

But not this time.

This time they were going to get a run for their money.

The big bus rolled forward across a rubble-strewn wasteland as searchlights picked it out, the roar of its engines blending with the wail of ricocheting 7.62-mm fleshrippers in a crescendo of death as the SCORF troops guarding the entrance whaled away with everything in their arsenal.

Two hundred yards.

DeLaCour manned the turret-mounted Minigun, blitzing out a hellstorm of rotoring lead. He scored a hit. Bullets raked the APC to the crash-bus's right.

The penetrator rounds pierced the weak spot just behind the troop carrier's door, beneath which was a bladder containing 50 gallons of highly combustible fuel.

Ka-booooom!

A massive fireball rose on a pillar of flame from the center of the kayoed APC. The vehicle disintegrated. Armor shards pinwheeled into the black night sky to a distance of 30 feet, then vortexed downward in a cascade of spinning shrapnel.

SCORF troopers who didn't take cover were sliced to bloody flayings. The men on the APC were blown to smithereens. Headless figures crawled and jerked in the final spasms of life as the flames consumed their screaming nervous systems.

One hundred yards.

Phoenix threw the clutch into fifth and savagely wrenched the steering wheel to veer suddenly from the path of two fast-moving HUMVEES which were screaming sharply from the right to cut the crash bus off.

The Greyhound juggernaut fishtailed and almost flipped over as it cut sharply left, and then right again, a hail of 7.62-mm penetrators stitching a zigzag of holes across the side of the bus's roof.

Raven let go of the MG she had been firing through the armored gunport on the Greyhound's rear, and hefted a LAW rocket tube from a crate on the bus's juddering deck.

Sighting on the closest of the two HUMVEEs, she triggered a HEAT warhead. The launcher belched fire and smoked as a lethal rocket streaked through the night on a luminous trail of sure destruction.

The HUMVEE driver tried to duck the incoming, but never had a chance. The high-mobility vehicle broke in half as one end went pinwheeling off into the HUMMER behind it, causing a second massive explosion.

The second vehicle's front end was blown straight across the sterile zone, flipping end-over-end before crashing into an APC across the way. The APC in turn exploded into a thousand berserkly spinning fragments. Strobing flames lit up the killzone as Phoenix screamed the bus past the burning wreckage, straight for the tunnel.

Impact!

Phoenix floored the gas, crashing the ten thousand pounds worth of Greyhound bus through the steel barricades directly in front of the mouth of the Lincoln Tunnel.

The armored battering ram mounted in front of the bus shattered the barricades like so much tinfoil. The bus screamed through, its engine roaring as it entered the tunnel.

Halogen floods mounted on the bus's roof and the sides bathed the interior of the tunnel in dazzling white light as Phoenix hit the stud to the left of the gas pedal.

Behind the bus, a motorized SCORF kill crew was already giving chase. Bullets spanged off the tarmac just behind the Greyhound's rear tires and bounced off its heavy armor plating.

"Heads up!" Phoenix screamed. He pulled a lever to his side. The battering ram dropped with a clank to the front of the Greyhound, sparking as the metal scraped asphalt at dizzying speed.

The battering ram was now a mine-catcher, detonating any mines or hurling them out of the way as the Greyhound barreled through the SCORF defense line.

The first mine they hit lifted the front of the bus a foot in the air as it went off, but the minesweeper and the armor plating on the Greyhound's underbelly kept damage to a minimum.

"Way to go!" screamed Raven from behind Trench at the back of the bus. Phoenix could see her flashing him the thumbs-up in the rearview.

At which point, the night exploded.

A HEAT rocket was streaking toward the Greyhound at point-blank range. It detonated a heartbeat later with enough force to almost rip the bus apart.

3

"I have visual contact now!" screamed the SCORF trooper in the first of the two armored firepods positioned at equidistant points along the length of the Lincoln Tunnel death corridor.

"Jesus! Look at that mother! It's got to be coming toward us at better than ninety!"

Constructed of stressed concrete lined with hardened steel plate, the heavily fortified gun emplacements were enormous hemispherical pillboxes, 30 feet in diameter, which hung from the tiled surface of the flat tunnel roof.

Crewed by three gunners each, the firepods were equipped with pintle-mounted .50 caliber Browning machine guns, each having a 180-degree fire field through semicircular gunports cut into either side of the firepods.

Circular ports dotting the firepod's surface were designed for man-portable LAW antiarmor rockets to be fired through.

Inside the firepods, the SCORF troopers were protected by shielding impervious to any but the most powerful armor-busting armament. They felt invincible and capable of wiping out anything that passed beneath them, no matter how big, heavily armored, or loaded with weaponry.

"Microwave the bus!" the voice from Tunnel Access Control crackled in the trooper's comset.

"Repeat! Destroy on sight!"

Fast-rotoring killfire belched suddenly from the muzzle of the Greyhound's roof-mounted Minigun as DeLaCour unleashed a white tornado of manbusting 7.62 blitzers at the firepod.

Hot sparks flew across the convex surface of Firepod One as the scorpion tails of full-auto death lashed furiously at it, leaving a trail of bulletholes but not piercing the heavily fortified armor of the SCORF gun emplacement.

Her M60 machine gun blazing and kicking in her fists, Raven pulled tailgunner duty, laying down a saturation line of autofire at the group of paramilitary HUMVEES which had chased the highballing Greyhound into the Lincoln Tunnel.

Now the Greyhound was close enough to Firepod One for the Browning greasegunner to see the face of the maniac up top with the Minigun.

The SCORF cowboy shuddered.

Half of the guy's face was made of stainless steel, glinting with a macabre brilliance as it caught the gleam of the overhead lights which lined the tunnel's roof.

Walking his fire across the armored roof of the Greyhound, the .50-caliber greasegunner was determined to nail the guy behind the M134 before he got out of range.

But the trooper was out of his league and he knew it. The armored shield protecting DeLaCour was too much even for the hardnose steeljackets which the Browning cranked out in ugly belches of stuttering flame.

The merc kept pouring on the full-auto heat anyway as the SCORF trooper beside him hunched down, hefted a LAW rocket tube to his shoulder, stuck its business end through one of the circular ports in the firepod, and sighted through the LAW's pop-up gunsight.

His strategy was to go for the wheelman. Take out the human guidance system of the steel-plated juggernaut below and it was game-over time for everybody inside. Simple and effective. This trooper was a merc who knew how to cut through the bullshit.

Getting the guy behind the Greyhound's steel-mesh windshield squarely between the rocket launcher's crosshairs, the trooper squeezed the trigger and felt the launcher buck in his fists as the bird left the pipe.

The HEAT warhead streaked from the rocket port of Firepod One and detonated with point-blank accuracy directly in front of the Greyhound's cab.

Try and walk away from that one, sucker, the merc thought.

WWWWWWWHUPPPPP!

A toadstool of broiling yellow flame erupted from the floor of the tunnel as the Greyhound swerved out of the path of a direct high-explosive strike in the midst of its kamikaze run.

Only a pulsebeat before, Magnus Trench had seen the ugly snout of the LAW tube protruding from the fire port and had guessed what was coming.

Screaming to DeLaCour and Raven to brace for a direct hit, Phoenix managed to turn the massive Greyhound coach so that the cab of the bus wouldn't take the burst head-on.

Instead of scoring a bullseye, the LAW strike sent its flame and molten shrapnel broadside of the fast-barreling bus, its shrapnel, concussive force, and heat deflected by the hardened armor plate riveted to the Greyhound's flanks.

Fighting for control of the wheel, Phoenix rode out the HEAT deathstorm as the force of the lethal blast was dissipated by the Greyhound's wraparound armor shielding.

The HEAT round kicked like a mule, though. It packed enough concussive power to slam the multi-ton armored vehicle against one of the tunnel's walls as though it were a child's toy.

Cords stood out on Phoenix's massive arms as he

fought the wheel to keep the bus steady. The Greyhound was still in imminent danger of flipping over and doing a crash and burn. Her brakes were locked by now and the bus was doing more skidding than rolling. The next few seconds would be critical to the survival of every one onboard.

Firepod One raked the roof and flanks of the careening crash vehicle with .50-caliber heat as it scraped the side of the tunnel's wall with a tooth-shivering banshee scream, sending out a hot shower of sparks before Phoenix could right the bus with a savage wrench of the wheel.

The scum guys from SCORF knew they had a 50-50 chance of taking out the bus. Each man in Firepod One was aware that a high-priority kill of this kind would mean instant field promotions for all of them. They'd be transferred out of the hellzone and into one of the western territories.

There were domes there, and inside the domes there were real trees and women without flashburns, radiation poisoning, and Plague lesions all over their bodies—and no Contams or radioactive snowstorms to contend with either.

That was enough motivation for any of the troopers in the firepod to risk his nuts to take out the fast-barreling Greyhound.

Each man opened up on the speeding road machine with everything they had.

WHAM!

Phoenix felt the shock from the base of his spine to the top of his head as the locked brakes sent the cab of the Greyhound slamming with bone-crushing impact against the tunnel wall, the impact lifting him off his seat and almost hurling him out of it.

Steering into the direction of the skid and trying to put the Greyhound on an even keel before it carommed off the opposite wall like some gargantuan pinball, Phoenix felt the locked brakes unfreeze slightly, giving him enough play in the steering to get the bus back under control.

Death continued to streak in a line of molten steel from the first firepod in front of the careening bus. DeLaCour was already bringing the M134 into fire position, swiveling the lethal weapon inside its circular cowling while Raven hefted her M60 machine gun and raked the pursuing SCORF crew with 7.62 blitzers.

The bus was now back on a reasonably straight heading.

In seconds it would be directly beneath the firepod, which was spraying bullets faster than swarms of angry hornets buzzing out of a threatened hive.

The heavy firepower spitting from the semicircular port was a problem, yeah, but Trench was more concerned about the circular ports to either side of the horizonal slit from which the machine gun's snout was delivering a lethal steel whirlwind.

The LAW strike that had almost kayoed the bus moments before had come from one of these. Phoenix sensed they only had seconds left before another HEAT warhead was launched their way. No armor would protect them from a direct hit at point-blank range. But the flipside of that equation, Phoenix was aware, was that the firepod would be a lot more vulnerable to a direct hit as well.

Stashed beside the Greyhound's driver's seat was an Uzi SMG with a rocket grenade threaded onto its barrel and ready for firing. Phoenix reached down, fisted the Uzi in his right hand and—taking his left off the wheel for a split second—pushed up the trap door of a gunport cut into the roof above him and squeezed the Uzi's trigger.

The pod exploded outwards, a cataract of flame and steel bathing the armored roof of the bus as the Greyhound barreled through the sudden wall of scorching fire.

Flame and body parts beat a tattoo on the roof as the

disintegrated remains of Firepod One tumbled past the Greyhound's armored windows in a jag-edged pyrotechnic cascade.

The Greyhound's minesweeper brushed aside wreckage strewing the bus's path as the bus cleared the killzone.

The first firepod's destruction allowed DeLaCour and Raven to return to dealing death at the SCORF chase crew which was hot on the bus's rear.

The fast-moving crew of heavily armored HUMVEEs was only a few car-lengths behind the crash vehicle. Flame ratcheted from the maws of the weapons mounted on the HUMVEEs.

Concentrated killfire from DeLaCour's and Raven's weapons took out the point HUMVEE. It exploded, spinning around and taking out another two pursuit cars. The rest screamed after the Greyhound, running over the burning bodies left in its wake.

Suddenly the Greyhound's halogens picked out two enormous steel plates appearing a few hundred yards ahead of the bus. At the Lincoln Tunnel's midpoint, one plate rose from the roadway while the other came swiftly down from the roof to meet it.

They would form an impenetrable barrier that would stop the bus dead in its tracks.

Hollering for DeLaCour and Raven to brace themselves for a crash, Phoenix triggered both of the Greyhound's front-mounted rocket tubes.

The HEAT missiles whooshed forward on twin streamers of billowing white smoke.

They exploded with thunderous impact against the steel-plate barrier, spattering the bus with splinters of shrapnel as the wall of hardened steel splintered into razor-edged confetti.

The momentum of the Greyhound's high-velocity run did the rest, and the bus was past the midpoint of the Lincoln Tunnel death run in seconds.

Now Phoenix could see the other end of the tunnel. Searchlight beams nervously crisscrossed the gaping mouth at its Manhattan end. Trench wiped a trickle of blood from a cut in his forehead from shrapnel that had penetrated the bus's shielding, and poured on more speed.

Just ahead was the second firepod, its merc crew already blazing away with every ounce of hardware they could muster.

DeLaCour was ready. Gripping the Minigun's spade grips, his index finger hooked on the M134's electrically operated triggers, he pumped a concentrated firestream at the firepod.

Whether it was luck, skill, or a combination of both, a burst of 7.62 whizzers penetrated the slit of the semi-circular machine-gun port. Bouncing around inside, they shredded human flesh and set off high-explosive munitions. The firepod went up in a broiling fireball that sent shock waves reverberating through the tunnel.

Now the tunnel's mouth loomed dead ahead. The bus had gained a solid lead on the pursuing HUMVEEs and was just a few hundred yards from entering Manhattan. Coming up fast was a cordon of SCORF vehicles forming a last-ditch barrier against the onrushing juggernaut.

Temporarily dropping their weapons, Raven and DeLaCour each lobbed a bundle of TNT behind the bus, their timers set for a three-second detonation lag.

The deafening explosion enveloped the tunnel in a corridor of fire as the Greyhound screamed through the mouth into the night, its rear fender barely clearing the cascade of rubble as the ceiling and the walls caved in.

HUMVEEs not reduced to burning trash or crushed by the tons of falling concrete wreckage were forced to turn back toward the tunnel's Jersey side.

Now Phoenix and crew turned their firepower on the SCORF troops in the sterile cordon on the Manhattan side.

Explosions lit up the wreckage on either side, strobing and flashing as the hellish light knifed through the night's indigo blackness.

The Greyhound was past the tunnel's final barricade now. Phoenix wrenched the wheel sending the bus screaming into the grid of streets to either side of the Lincoln Tunnel's mouth. After a series of breakneck turns at high speed, he stopped the bus and killed the engine.

"Shake it!" Trench hollered, jumping from behind the seat and shouldering the pack of supplies stowed behind it as Raven and DeLaCour did the same from their ends.

In seconds, they knew, the SCORF pursuers would be down the street they'd stopped on, hellbent on obliterating their targets.

No sooner had the trio hustled for the cover of wreckage surrounding the street than the HUMVEE kill crew screamed around the corner.

But a surprise was waiting for the hit paraders. A surprise that would—literally—blow them away.

Phoenix paused a beat, then punched the black button on the radio-controlled detonator he held in his hand, a grim smile playing across his granite features.

Nestled inside the Greyhound, enough C-4 explosives to raze a skyscraper went off with a deafening explosion as the motorized chase crew got well within the blast's lethal radius.

Secondary explosions marked the places where the HUMMERS were blown to hell as munitions onboard went up with savage concussive hammer blows.

"Okay," Phoenix said when the dust had cleared, revealing burning debris scattered as far as the eye could see.

"Let's get serious."

4

Liberty Island.

By some macabre oversight of destiny it had been spared the fate of the rest of the City of Nuked York.

Manhattan Island was little better than a volcanic cinder cone of twisted, blackened wreckage.

Most of Brooklyn and Queens had been reduced to piles of charred rubble filled with the nauseating stench of millions of rotting corpses.

Staten Island and the Bronx were slagheaps, their cores still semi-molten. The Soviet nukes which had blitzed the city had opened previously unknown seismic faults in the crust of the earth.

The Bronx was now an earthquake zone as unstable as the San Andreas Fault. Poison clouds of steam belched from jagged scars in the ground, and rivers of molten lava flowed over the busted streets.

The Statue of Liberty still stood.

Firestorms which had burned for weeks just across the East River in Manhattan had coated the 600-foot copper statue with a thick layer of soot and grime so that her familiar blue-green patina had turned into a dull black.

But Lady Liberty herself was still intact. Her right hand, bearing a 30-foot torch, was still held aloft, while in her left, a gigantic book was carried.

But the torch had not been lit since the night before the world ended in nuclear hellfire, and the inscription chiseled into the metal pages of the book which Lady Liberty clutched against her breast had been blotted out by the destructive aftermath of a nuclear firestorm.

Men had come to Liberty Island after the fires of destruction had cooled in the nuked city across the river.

They had hovered, then touched down in military rotorcraft, embarking on the island's grounds in radiation-shielded suits which filtered the cancer-causing dust particles in the air. Inside the suits, the men who had emerged from the copters resembled astronauts from some other planet.

They were the Dark Messiah's soldiers of scum, members of Luther Enoch's mercenary army which policed the Urban Containment Zones of CONUS, the Continental United States.

They were the shock troops of the new, but not better, U.S.-NCSC Government, a marriage between Church and State which combined the most corrupt parts of both in an unholy union.

A union that had its roots in the warped mind of the greatest mass murderer in human history, Luther Enoch, the Dark Messiah.

Enoch had believed that only nuclear Armageddon could destroy what he considered a Satanic American society by blasting it to smithereens.

In the power vacuum that would be left behind, Enoch would create a New Order. It would be populated by the Dark Messiah's followers, his mind-thralls whom he programmed in orgies of sex and drug-induced brainwashing.

By staging the assassination of the President, then faking a full-scale Soviet missile launch which would trick NORAD computers into launching a retaliatory strike, Enoch had engineered the nuclear death spasm which would crucify America on a fiery cross.

And while the firestorms raged above ground, the Dark Messiah's merc army and his mindfucked followers both would be protected in a multi-billion-dollar network of nuclear-resistant bomb shelters across the nation, ready to emerge and take control after the war was over.

That's just what they did.

Without a soul to stop them.

The first thing the Dark Messiah's troops did was to seal off the blasted-to-hell cities of America behind an airtight cordon of mercenary troops.

In some cases, like St. Louis and Chicago, enormous walls had been raised around the cities, like those of medieval feudal states. They became Urban Containment Zones or UCZs. They were used as vast concentration camps for the diseased and destitute survivors of the terminal nuclear blitz.

At first, Enoch had intended on mass slaughter.

But then he realized the millions of survivors pent up in the madhouses of the UCZs would be necessary as a source of organs to sustain the lives of the Dark Messiah's New Order. There had been exposure to an unknown Soviet supervirus called Plague.

Plague which slowly changed the infected into mindless, bloodthirsty ghouls called Contams.

Presiding over the ruined cities was the job of SCORF, the Special Commando Retaliatory Force, an elite paramilitary brigade made up of the cream of the Dark Messiah's military forces and under the command of John Tallon, Enoch's merc enforcer.

SCORF had come to Liberty Island and begun digging the warren of concrete corridors, heavily fortified command, control, and intelligence bunkers and high-tech disease-control laboratories which honeycombed the island like some obscene hive of monster termites.

The Dark Messiah's military engineers had constructed a concrete retaining wall around the island 30 feet in height. Dotted with machine-gun emplacements, the wall completely surrounded the island, rendering it impervious to attack.

Powerful searchlights could pinpoint any invading craft, and Apache helos could be immediately dispatched to blast attackers right out of the water.

From SCORF's Liberty Island hardbase, the Dark Messiah's troops commanded the charred and flash-melted remains of the Nuked Apple.

SCORF elite forces garrisoned within the scorched and nuke-blasted metropolitan area were under the control of the Liberty Island hardbase at all times.

Their primary mission: *bug hunts.*

Bug hunts referred to the regular population-control sweeps in which the denizens of mashed Manhattan Island were flushed from their hiding places beneath the rubble and rounded up by the hundreds.

The prisoners of SCORF population-control sweeps were then transported by ferry across the East River to Liberty Island, destined for the dissection rooms of the Liberty Base disease-control laboratory, where their organs would be surgically removed from their anesthetized bodies, flash frozen, and flown to points across the smashed ruins of America for implantation in the diseased bodies of the Dark Messiah's elite.

Those prisoners not dissected immediately would be killed and stored in a gigantic freezer in the bowels of Liberty Base for later dissection.

Hundreds of battle-ready troops were garrisoned on the hardbase, ready to be instantly deployed to counter any uprising from the boroughs beyond. Not that many were likely.

In every borough but Brooklyn—where the badass warlord calling himself Abraxas had rallied thousands of war survivors into a self-contained society with its center in the housing projects of Coney Island—little better than a state of total chaos prevailed.

In these savage hotzones, it was every man for himself. Winner took all and the loser wound up dead, his corpse quickly stripped to the bones by human and animal scavengers alike.

Ordinarily the scavs gave the Dark Messiah's troopers

little trouble—except for the occasional breakout attempt, which would be punished by massive retaliation. Most nights, Liberty Base was kept on a state of minimum alert.

But not tonight.

Tonight something was happening.

Something special.

Tonight fires burned in the mid-Manhattan hellzone across the open sewer on the East River. Communications sweeps were pouring data into the Liberty Island hardbase's command-and-control bunker with mind-blowing speed. Pure fucking chaos had taken possession of the streets of the city across the waters of the river.

Instead of trying to break out of Nuked York City, somebody was trying to bust their way in!

John Tallon strode into the command-and-control center, the steady cadence of the polished jackboots worn over the black pants of his elite commando uniform cracking like pistol shots on the polished tile floor.

At their banks of screens all around the immense circular room, soldiers in military camo fatigues sat and manned the flashing readouts, which delivered constantly updated information on the status of the pitched firefight at the Lincoln Tunnel as Phoenix and company made a mockery of the SCORF Access Control force.

Tallen tapped one of the soldiers on the shoulder. The comlink operator stiffened when he saw the blacksuited merc honcho with the Mauser slung across his chest.

"What's the status of the operation?" Tallon asked the kid.

"Telemetry's just coming in from Fury Team now, sir," the comlink man returned. "Want me to put it on the screen?"

At Tallon's curt nod, the console in front lit up with a series of rapidly painted characters of green light:

F L A S H

Tallon/NEDTZ UCZ/D2XR/Code X/11-09W

BT/////////////////

QUADRANT THREE REPORTS INITIAL CONTACT . . . .

QUADRANTS FOUR, FIVE, AND SIX NOT YET SECURE. . . .

VEHICLES OF ALL CONFIGURATIONS DESTROYED BY INVADING FORCE»ARMORED COACH BREACHED BARRIERS AT LINCOLN TUNNEL 0:335 HRS TO MAKE FORCED ENTRY INTO MANHATTAN ISLAND CONTROL SECTOR CHARLIE-TROJAN-ZULU»»PURSUIT AND INTERCEPTION TEAM DIAMOND IMMEDIATELY MOVED TO INTERCEPT AND/OR DESTROY TARGET VEHICLE RESULTING IN THE LOSS AND DESTRUCTION OF AT LEAST THREE APCS AND AN AS-YET-UNKNOWN NUMBER OF HUMVEES»»THE NUMBER OF DEAD CANNOT YET BE DETERMINED DUE TO MASSIVE DISMEMBERMENT OF TERMINAL CASUALTIES»»STANDING BY FOR FURTHER ORDERS»»

EOM///////////////

"Should I instruct Fury Team to continue pursuit?" asked the comlink officer.

Tallon stood and stared off into space, an unreadable expression in his eyes, as though he were watching a drama unfold a million light years away.

"Sir?"

"*Negative,*" Tallon finally snapped at the young officer. "Instruct all units to resume regular patrol."

"But, sir," the comlink officer interjected, "that means the intruders will be able to—"

Tallon cut the shavetail off with a wave of his black-gloved hand. His fingertips rested lightly on the butt of the World-War-Two-vintage Mauser nested in a pit holster across his chest like a viper in its lair.

A strained tension filled the room. Tallon had blown men away for not instantly obeying an order.

"I know goddamn well what that means, soldier," he told the green marine in a razor-edged voice. "Now carry out the command."

Swallowing hard, the soldier did as he was told.

It had finally sunk in not to argue with the man who held life-or-death power over him.

He was relieved when Tallon finally stalked out of the command bunker.

The shavetail was green.

Too green to even realize how close he had come to filling a six-foot hole in the ground.

5

Describe the city.

You can't.

Words fail you. Your mind reels at the horror of the devastation which spreads as far as the eye can see.

Looking around you, you can almost hear the screams of the dying millions as the flesh bubbled on their bones and the blood spurted in sizzling jets from their ears and eyes in their final terror-filled moments on the gone-insane planet.

You can almost feel the bone-crushing force of the 60-megaton nuclear shock waves which leveled concrete-and-steel skyscrapers like so many dominoes and caved in the subway tunnels like spades crushing the burrows of earthworms, which tore human beings limb-from-limb, which maimed and mutilated those who survived, and which split the earth like so much brittle icing on a cake to burst the water, gas, and electrical mains running beneath it, feeding the howling firestorm with even more fuel.

You feel like you're about to go insane. Tears of rage and impotent frustration are streaming from your eyes despite the throbbing in your heart that makes you grit your teeth in righteous anger. Your knees buckle and your gut starts to heave as your body shakes from the sheer, raw horror of this stinking cesspool the crazy fuckers have made of your world.

You want to vomit, oh, sweet Jesus, you want to bend over, grab your guts, open your mouth, and puke your fucking insides out. The utter, terminal devastation seen all around you is sickening beyond comprehension.

None of this will ever be the way it was again! It's all gone forever, a thing raped and killed and lying under the dying sun devoured by obscene, slime-dripping maggots that crawl through its twisted metal guts and shit all over its broken concrete soul and fester in its smashed and ruptured heart.

A nauseating stench, made up in equal parts of the lingering smell of rotting flesh and charred, decaying skeletons and of scorched metal and burned brick, permeates the air; you can almost feel it covering your body like a thin plastic bag. Cold sweat breaks out all over you as you struggle to keep your mind and body under tight control.

You know that if you lose it for even a second, you'll freak out, go totally apeshit berserk. You've seen it happen to others in Nam—go "dinky dau," as the gooks called it—and you know how it ended for them: with a burst from the bushes that took off their heads, with a Cong booby trap that impaled them against a tree on a giant bamboo stake.

You know that what you see around you can drive any man over the brink of madness into the eternal hell that lies just beyond.

It is the ultimate madness, the terminal folly of a race of mentally diseased and spiritually unclean beings, a race of stunted pygmies convinced they were gods, doomed to extinction by its own violent hand since its half-animal ancestors crawled out of the flickering shadows of a savage prehistory a million years before.

Yet you must. You must look around you even though the madness lingers in the brain even when the eyes are closed, the images flickering even in sleep, burned into every dark crack and crevice of your mind. You have to take it all in, because if you don't, there's no way you'll survive.

Images . . .

Broadway. Funky, funky, Broadway. Down on Broadway, there's a madness, name of the madness—nuclear destruction.

Where skyscrapers once soared in arrogant challenge to the sky, there is now nothing but blackened, twisted, flashmelted wreckage. The hulks of rusting cars, buses, and trucks, piled like cordwood one atop the other, choke the side streets feeding onto the city's most storied artery, the largest street in the world, the blood-caked lifeline which ran straight to its heart.

Mummified remains, bare skeletons picked clean by profane scavengers, are contained inside the trashed vehicles like mummified Pharaohs inside sarcophagi.

A crosstown bus lies on its side, skeletons hanging out its windows, the death figures in hideous freeze frame while trying to escape as the Soviet airbursts detonated above the doomed city.

By Herald Square, a gigantic crevasse runs from Thirty-fourth Street down Broadway as far as the eye can see. Vehicles of every shape, size, and description litter the bottom of the yawning fissure, and more skeletons are jumbled in the mass grave.

Then something moves. Out of the corner of your eye, you see it. A shadow, a flicker. You spin, simultaneously bringing your weapon into firing position, but by then it's gone. You continue hauling ass through the wreckage, feeling unseen eyes on your back.

Waiting.

Watching.

Rounding a corner you hear a gnashing sound, growling everywhere from many throats. The horror hits you like a sledgehammer. A pack of wild dogs clusters around the body of a naked woman lying in the street.

Although her body has been ripped open from throat to pubis, the woman is still alive enough to weakly try to push away the savage animals which are devouring her.

Not that it's doing her any good.

They are ripping out her entrails, tearing them out in long, gleaming strips of wet, bloody flesh, their snouts covered with gore as they dip in and out of the gaping carcass, chewing and chomping down their grisly feast. One roots down in the bloody opening and comes up with the woman's heart, still beating and squirting redness from the tubes dangling from it as the animal scarfs it down. Another tears the cunt off and bolts down the hairy pelt, belching with satisfaction.

Then you're hit with the punchline. It's not dogs you see.

Rats.

You're looking at enormous mutant rats.

It's only the beginning.

Times Square.

Trashed to hell though it is, you still recognize it.

Automotive wreckage is everywhere. Buses overturned, lying half in and half out of the remains of the shops on every side. Theatre marquees smashed to pieces and lying in the wreckage-strewn streets.

Traffic must have been heavy when the Soviet nukebursts detonated.

Further up Broadway, where it merges with the Avenue of the Americas. More chaos. You remembered it as a manmade canyon, concrete towers reaching for the sun as if daring the gods to stop mankind's quest for perfection.

Mankind.

Puny, nothing mankind. A race of dwarves which believed it could become like gods. A race of fools. A race which lit the match to its own eternal hell.

Thermonuclear detonations of more than 60 megatons had blasted midtown Manhattan with incredible force.

Steel beams had snapped like matchsticks. Concrete losts its strength, ran like molten jelly. Steel liquified and mixed with the carbonized flesh of the millions of victims cremated in the first few seconds of destruction.

Hundreds of millions of tons of wreckage turned to

burning dust. A column of superheated cinders rose 60 miles into the stratosphere. More lives than had died in Hitler's ovens were snuffed out in a heartbeat of time.

Airbursts at sea caused massive tidal waves which flooded the subway tunnels beneath the dying city. Trapped. They were trapped down there like insects.

Millions of them, screaming in mind-searing horror as they drowned in the crippled trains in the city's constipated bowels.

Firestorms came.

Crackling, seething flame walked the streets of Manhattan like a striding colossus, a monster hotter than the surface of the sun which obliterated everything it touched. Fire consumed what the blast had left standing. It scorched the denuded, flashmelted girders still erect against a fever sky.

The firestorm's unimaginable temperatures made the asphalt run like melted butter. It penetrated every crevice of the city, fumigating them with millions of cubic feet of toxic smoke to kill the hunkering denizens who cowered like human rats in the basements of demolished skyscrapers.

And when it was over, when the fires had died and the air was no longer filled with the thunder of the nukes and the screams of the victims of Armageddon, the survivors of apocalypse realized the terrible truth.

Hell had just begun.

All around them was a wasteland. A wasteland which had come into being from the twisted nightmare of mankind's deepest secret places where terror howls and gibbers and reality is a waking dream.

It was the world in which they would now live. And die.

It was the world their ancestors had left behind in the savage dawn of creation.

It was the world their leaders had bequeathed them in the savage night of mankind's final days on earth.

It was the world in which the savages ruled.

Welcome to that world . . .

"You getting the same feeling I'm getting?" asked DeLaCour of Phoenix. With Trench on point, flanked by the steel-faced giant and Raven, they cautiously threaded their way up Sixth Avenue toward the Upper East Side.

"Like you're a string of salami hanging on a hook in a butcher's window?" Trench returned.

"Yeah, exactly," returned DeLaCour.

They were now approaching the remains of Radio City Music Hall. The marquee had been knocked to the street. They turned down Forty-ninth Street toward Rockefeller Center.

"Damn it!" Raven suddenly cried out.

She didn't have to add another syllable.

All around them, the rubble exploded as the jibbering denizens of Nuked York City sprang from their hiding places.

Rags hung on the bodies of the scavs, and most of them brandished crude weapons which would have been no match for the fully automatic firearms Phoenix and the team carried.

But the scavs had the numbers. There seemed to be hundreds of them, as though they had sprouted from the wreckage like soldiers sown from dragons' teeth.

They were led by leather badasses wielding heavy firepower, though. And all of them were out for blood.

Without warning the rubble erupted around Phoenix's feet as a hail of autofire kicked up the garbage. The scum battalion of terminal men was on the warpath, hellbent on tearing the intruders limb-from-limb.

"Disturbance. Sector Zulu Specter Niner."

"Roger, Zebra-Four, we copy."

"Instructions?"

"Proceed with the sweep, Zebra-Four. Whatever it is

just makes it easier to herd the scav fuckers."

"We copy that, Leader Bravo. Proceeding with sweep. Zebra-Four out."

"What the hell you think stirred the scum people up?"

"Don't know, don't care. It's just another run far as I'm concerned, Kemo Sabe. Soon as we get those Injuns down there corralled, I'm due for some R&R time. Can almost taste some cold brew and hot pussy."

"Yeah, hear they got some clean ones in from the Northern Territories. No flashburns, hardly no Plague. Clean and sweet."

"I like the mutes. Like to feel the way some of 'em got scales all over their bods. Their tits especially. You ever fuck a mute? Ever fuck the kind with two cunts, four tits, eyes in the back of their heads?"

"I screwed a scav woman once. She gave good head."

"Ain't nowhere near the same. Mutes are somethin' else, partner. Mutes give you—"

"Damn! *You see that?*"

"Sure, crushed that fucker right under the forward leg."

"Yeah. Right underneath. Shit, I love that when it happens."

"Well, just hang on, good buddy. You're gonna see a lot more of that soon as we get to the sweep zone."

6

A badass in a black cycle jacket and a coonskin cap clutched his ruptured chest and vomited up a piece of his heart. The .45 pistol clattered from his hands to the rubble at his feet as Coonskin did a spastic boogaloo and pitched onto his face.

Phoenix pivoted quickly from the first kill, sighting the M60 machine gun on another target. Wearing a Nazi helmet and a sheepskin vest, this scuzzbag was fisting an Ingram SMG in each hand, laughing and hollering as he blazed away with a dual autofire blitzkrieg.

Ducking under the crosshail of heavy-caliber death, Phoenix rolled and came up firing from a crouch. Although an awkward firing position, it got the job done—a 7.62-mm slug caught the crude dude in the thigh, fragmented on the hip bone, and buzzsawed around inside him, ripping apart his guts in the process. As Sheepskin stumbled sideways, Phoenix blew his head off with a mercy burst that was better than the punk deserved.

DeLaCour and Raven had their own hands full as the scav attack went down full-fury.

The steel-faced guy from New Orleans was single-handedly taking out a human-wave attack of ragged scum people armed with makeshift clubs and other crude, though deadly, weapons.

Armed with an M16A2 assault rifle, Raven dodged a

storm of lead tumblers and took cover behind a large, jagged heap of melted slag which had once been the statue of Atlas supporting the world on his shoulders at Rock Center. She opened fire and caught two scavs across the chest, stitching them from throat to belly with 5.56-mm softnose rounds.

With the first wave of casualties, the attack's tempo slacked off. For a few minutes the corpse-littered hell-ground was silent as the scav bushwackers melted back into the woodwork. They quickly regrouped, though, and came forward again, more ferociously than before.

Phoenix and DeLaCour hotfooted it out of harm's way. Back-to-back, they unleashed a wave of autofire at the blood-crazed scavs. Raven pitched two grenades.

Dual explosions made mincemeat of a brace of club-wielding skirmishers. The rest ran from the sites of the carnage. The denizens of the wasteland had finally realized that the numbers didn't mean much in the face of superior fighting skill.

The attack melted away as rapidly as it had materialized.

Phoenix stared at the heaps of wreckage which rose like miniature hills in the Valley of the Shadow of Death. *This* is where it had been. He could feel it in his bones. God, how the memories assaulted his brain.

Home.

Gone.

A building had once stood here. A silver high-rise jutting 60 stories into the air above the bustling Upper East Side of Manhattan.

Now there was only the foul stench of smoldering wreckage, the tumult of screams from the deathlands beyond, the maddening sight of the mangled remains of another reality that was now mutilated beyond all recognition.

DeLaCour shook his head at Raven.

"Leave him," he whispered, throwing a massive arm

around her shoulder. "Let him make his peace with the dead."

But there was no peace for Magnus Trench. Only madness. Phoenix threw back his head and screamed, assaulted by memories which struck at his brain like hammer blows, he pointed his weapon at the sky and fired a long, thundering 7.62 autoburst until the 100-round box mag ran dry.

Flinging the useless weapon to the rubble, Trench stumbled dazedly through the destruction that had once been his home, picturing the street as it once had been.

A line of brownstone row houses had stood on the north side of the street. Small specialty shops and several good restaurants lined the broad expanse of Second Avenue. Nearby had been the school his young son had attended. All day long there was the noisy ebb and flow of traffic, and at night the headlights of cars would send spokes of brilliance whirling through the slats of the drawn venetians.

Magnus Trench wished he had died on that September afternoon when the Soviet nukebursts had annihilated his future and that of countless millions of other Americans. But instead, he had been spared. Why? he wondered. Why him above so many others?

He had been three thousand miles from home, on the other side of the continent, on a redwood-studded mountaintop in the Muir Woods National Forest overlooking San Francisco Bay when the nukes had exploded.

Trench had gone there for three days of solitude in the wilderness after wrapping up a multimillion dollar deal for Conrex, the company he represented as a corporate troubleshooter.

Three days which were to have replenished his spirit, cleansed his soul, recharged his mental batteries. After which he was to have flown back to New York, returned to spend a final week with his family before going back to the nine-to-five grind.

But Magnus Trench never got back to his family or his desk. Instead the unthinkable had happened. The orgasmic moment of world-obliterating destruction would never leave Trench's mind. It was permanently etched there, like an obscenity chiseled for eternity into stone.

Magnus Trench had climbed the steep side of the mountain to his camp in the pristine redwood forest of the National Parkland. He had cooked his dinner and sat looking out over the sparkling waters of San Francisco Bay. Pleasure craft were sailing, and the setting sun as it glinted off the windshields of cars passing over the Golden Gate Bridge made the traffic stream seem like a diamond river.

Airburst!

A 20-megaton Soviet fireball exploded directly over downtown San Francisco, so hellishly bright that it eclipsed the setting sun. Trench turned his eyes from the luminous face of thermonuclear holocaust. Knowing he had only seconds before the blast wave reached him, he hauled ass for the shelter of the cave at which he'd made camp, burrowing in like a human mole with as many supplies as he could grab.

For the next 48 hours, Trench had huddled in the womb of living rock, listening to the firestorm howling around him like a million banshees, hearing in his mind the screams of the countless dead and dying in the doomed city below him and all across America.

His brain reeled with the awful knowledge that San Francisco was not the only American city reduced to ashes by the nukes. Trench knew that New York was hit as well, and had probably taken the first strike. Worst of all, he knew that his family was swept up in the tide of death that had suddenly and without warning rolled across the land.

Two days after Apocalypse, Magnus Trench, the corporate troubleshooter, had emerged from his hiding place into a bizarre terminal deathscape of jagged stumps that had once been the tallest trees in the world.

Chemical smog floated eerily over the wasteland of the Muir Woods. Beyond the cave, at the crest of the mountainside, Trench looked down on the mass graveyard which the city of San Francisco had become.

And Phoenix was reborn.

Phoenix.

The mythic bird which all ancient cultures revered as a symbol of resurrection, but which was especially sacred to the Vietnamese who called it the Phung Hoang.

Magnus Trench had been the Phung Hoang, years before. He had moved like a shadow through the jungles of Vietnam, killing in a thousand ways, becoming a man both feared and respected by U.S. forces and North Vietnamese alike.

Phoenix.

A warrior with the image of the Phung Hoang tattooed above his heart as an ancient Chinese mark of courage. A warrior who had put aside his lethal prowess to assume the mantle of civilian life. A warrior who was reborn in the death and madness and mindbending chaos of the thermonuclear holocaust.

A man with one goal and one alone: rejoin his family if they still lived and exact terrible vengeance on the man who he had learned had orchestrated the nightmarish destruction of his world and everything in it: Luther Enoch, the Dark Messiah.

The man called Phoenix had set out on his search, venturing down into the deathlands of San Francisco, then to Las Vegas, and across the ravaged country to St. Louis and the Gulf states, always coming closer, yet somehow never any nearer to his ultimate goal. *Nuked York City.*

And now he was here. Finally.

And all that was left was wreckage.

But Phoenix still didn't know what he'd come to the mass graveyard of Manhattan Island to find out. Somehow he was certain that his family was still alive. *Somehow.* There was no way to tell for sure, though. Not here, anyway.

Magnus Trench picked up the M60. Walking from the heap of wreckage that had once been his home, he rejoined DeLaCour and Raven.

"Let's get out of here," he said, not even trying to hide the tears streaking his face.

The three Armageddon warriors stalked through the chaos. Daylight was waning. The red ball of the post-nuclear sun cast long, eerie shadows across the trashed wasteland around them.

Walking westward, toward the river, they came to a flat expanse that had once been a city housing project. Now it was a vast amphitheater.

Movement.

From all sides another group of scavs appeared. Blood was in their eyes. They had regrouped in even greater numbers. They would not leave the skirmish site without victims this time.

No matter how many of them were cut down in the process, they were determined not to leave empty-handed.

Phoenix, DeLaCour, and Raven all sensed this. And they realized it was a fight which they might not walk away from. The sheer numbers were too much. They were overwhelmed.

A group of scavs brandishing makeshift weapons moved first, dozens running at the three outsiders, who were quickly encircled with no cover and no place to retreat to.

Phoenix, DeLaCour, and Raven opened up with everything they had. Bodies dropped. But others ran out over the corpses in their paths, hollering and gnashing their teeth.

Suddenly, there was thunder.

The scavs looked up, frightened out of their wits.

An apparition from hell had appeared over the wreckage. It rose on four enormous steel legs which shook the earth as the multi-ton machine strode across the skirmish zone.

At the front of its steel body was a windowed cab. Men could be seen inside it, working the steel beast's navigation controls and computerized weapons system. The insignia on it told everything.

It bore the mark of the US-NCSC Government, a triad of interlocking sevens. The sign of the Beast. It was a SCORF Strider—or PLV, for Pedal Locomotion Vehicle—an advanced-design all-terrain vehicle specially developed for use in the uneven terrain of the UCZs which made even tracked APCs almost useless.

Autofire spurted from the twin MK5.50-caliber Gatlings mounted on pods to either side of the Strider's cab. Dozens of scavs were quickly cut down. The rest broke and ran away from the Strider.

They were driven right into a squad of heavily armed men in paramilitary fatigues. The troops packed automatic weapons. Behind them was an APC, into which the scavs were thrown after being pistol-whipped or shot in the legs.

Phoenix had seen SCORF operations in enough UCZs to know what was happening. An organ raid. The scavs were being rounded up as they were routinely across the country.

Their bodies would be picked clean in the laboratories of the Dark Messiah. Their body tissues and their genes would be studied under microscopes.

Others would be infected with the Plague virus and turned into Contams, before being killed and flash-frozen.

Yeah, the hardware was unfamiliar, but the name of the game was always the same.

Phoenix looked around hastily for a safe corridor out of the melee, but could see none. To make matters worse, a couple of SCORF hardguys had spotted the trio. Phoenix could see them pointing and gesturing, then grab a HUMVEE and split off from the main platoon. The HUMMERized hit crew took off through the swirling cordite smoke straight at them.

"Suck dirt! On the double!"

From one of the narrow alleys leading to the square, Phoenix saw a sight he couldn't believe.

It was a Checker Cab.

The taxi was honking its horn frantically as it highballed their way. With a screech of tires, it pulled up and the shotgun-side door was thrown open.

Phoenix jumped in back, pulling Raven after him while DeLaCour jumped in beside the driver.

"Where to, Cochise?" asked the driver at DeLaCour. Dark-lensed Wayfarers hid the dude's eyes, and a tangle of dreadlocks nearly hid his face, the black coils spilling down over the back of the iridescent blue kung fu-jacket he wore. The Checker had the words "Li'l Stinky" painted in flowing script across both yellow flanks.

"Hell!" screamed DeLaCour in answer.

"Got news for you, m'man," the cabbie shot back, "you're already there."

"Just move, damn you!" Phoenix yelled. "And fast."

"Hey, no problem, amigo," returned the cabbie, unperturbed by the war wagons barreling toward them at breakneck speed while autofire ratcheted from their machine guns.

With that, he pulled a fast bootlegger, turning the Checker in a full circle in just under a second. Hitting a stud beneath the dashboard, the cabbie sent a HEAT warhead screaming from a rocket tube concealed beneath the rear fender of the Checker.

The HUMVEE exploded in a broiling phallus of fiery destruction as the Checker bolted away into the gathering darkness, twisting and turning through a mazelike labyrinth of streets.

"That first rocket's free," the cabbie said over his shoulder once they'd safely cleared the firezone. "Any more costs you extra."

7

"Bush Doctor don't usually go this deep into the scum zone," the cabbie said as he expertly whipped the Checker through a grid of busted streets. "Only work the better neighborhoods."

Phoenix recognized some of these streets from his past life in New York. Others were paths across stretches of urban wasteland which had never existed until after N-Day.

"But Bush Doctor knew something heavy was going down," continued the cabbie, "picking up some fucking serious transmission activity from Liberty Island."

He pointed at the center of the Checker's dash, which was loaded with an array of sophisticated-looking electronics.

Phoenix exchanged glances with DeLaCour and Raven. The situation had gone from incredibly bad to impossibly weird. He had been prepared to accept a lot of strange revelations in the ashes of Nuked York. But a crazy Rastafarian driving a Checker Cab wasn't one of them.

Yet that's just what was happening. The trio was being hustled with incredible speed through the rubble-strewn, torchlit nightworld of Manhattan Island. Their destination, though, was still unknown.

"Where in hell are we going?" Phoenix asked the cabbie.

"Where you want to go?" Bush Doctor returned. "The meter's running."

"Somewhere safe," said DeLaCour. "Somewhere we can hole up for awhile."

"Know just the place," the cabbie said. "You be safe as a Bible at a hooker convention."

They fell silent for the rest of the drive, which continued at the same breakneck pace as the earlier part of it.

The cabbie seemed to know where every bottleneck, every debris-choked street, every ambush point where armed scavengers waited to strike in the blitzed boro of trashed Manhattan was located, and effortlessly evaded them all.

The cab finally screamed around a corner and down a narrow curb cut. Bush Doctor whipped a small remote unit from his pocket and a heavy steel door slid up into the wall. The cab zoomed down a narrow incline, and there was the sound of the steel door sliding back down again to lock with a solid thud.

"It ain't much," the cabbie said, switching off the ignition and cracking open his door, "but I call it home." He got out, stretched, and ran a plastic pick through his coils of dreadlocks. Phoenix, DeLaCour, and Raven followed suit, climbing out of the Checker and uncramping their arms and legs.

They were inside a large underground space bordered by walls of naked concrete, the ceiling supported by massive concrete beams positioned everywhere and illuminated dimly by bulbs in cages, probably powered by a gas generator chugging away in a corner. The place looked and smelled like a garage.

"Trump Tower above got flattened," the cabbie said by way of explanation, "but the garage, it stayed together. Bush Doctor call this place home. Nobody know about it."

"You get many fares these days?" asked Raven.

"You my first this week," Bush Doctor replied, adding, "but I got a tradition to uphold. I come from a long line of cabbies. You know that scene in *Midnight Cowboy* where Ratso kicks the cab? Well, the cabbie was my cousin Twango. What you think of that?"

Nobody answered. They were too busy staring.

"Well anyway," Bush Doctor finally said, "there gonna be chow ready soon, if you want it."

The cabbie led them up a flight of stairs into a second level of the garage that had been outfitted as crude living quarters. A refrigerator hummed against a wall.

Weapons and ammunition were stacked in a corner of this area. Electronics equipment, probably heisted from looted stores, was stacked against another wall. Computers and character printers of all types were visible there.

"We gonna chow down now," the cabbie said. He dug into the fridge and pulled out a stiff dog carcass.

"Fresh one," he said with a smile. "Caught it the other day on Fourteenth Street. Got it stuffed with rat meat."

The Rememberer lived in what had once been an underground pumping station of the Sewer Department. The pump room was near the river. The Hudson was cold and gray, its waters reflecting the sinking red blob of the sun.

"Gotta be cool around the Rememberer," cautioned Bush Doctor. "Rememberer very choosy about who she talks to. You let Bush Doctor make the introductions, okay?"

Phoenix followed the cabby down a flight of moldy concrete stairs. Torches smoked on the walls in iron sconces. At the bottom, where there was a small, cavernous room, Trench saw an old hag dressed in filthy rags hunched over a screen which cast a flickering green glow on her ravaged face.

"Rememberer," Bush Doctor began, approaching the hag. "Brought you some folks need your services."

The hag looked up. In the light of the screen it was apparent that the woman wasn't old, she was just diseased. Plague blisters festered on a face that had aged prematurely due to the brutal conditions under which she survived. Her hair was white and pulled back into two long braids.

The eyes were dead, though. Blind white orbs which saw nothing. Eyes that were melted, Phoenix knew, melted in the moment of revelation when hell came down to earth in searing thermonuclear blast waves.

On the flickering screen into which she stared were meaningless zigzags which flickered and strobed as they passed across the glass surface of the picture tube. The blind woman stared into the sightless television eye in her darkened cavern.

Suddenly the woman jerked her head up from the screen before which she had been rocking in a catatonic trance. Her mouth opened revealing her toothless gums. An insane shriek escaped her lips coming from deep in her throat. She began laughing and gibbering dementedly.

"Don't let the Rememberer freak you out," advised Bush Doctor. "She just don't like strangers, is all." The cabbie put his hands on the madwoman's shoulders and eased her back into the chair.

"Rememberer," he exclaimed, "get your shit together. This man I brought have got a problem. He looking for his wife and son. You gotta help the dude, hear?"

"What are the names?" the young-old woman croaked in a voice that sounded like it had come from beyond the grave. "Tell me the names."

"Trench," said Phoenix in a soft voice. "Sandra and Brian. My wife and son."

The woman's eyes rolled up inside her head. She began rocking back and forth again, humming softly to herself in a bizarre monotone while the muscles in her neck and face twitched and jerked.

"Rememberer working on it," the cabbie explained

with a touch of pride in his voice. "She's something else, ain't she?"

The cabbie told Phoenix that the Rememberer had once been a Congresswoman. People came to her after N-Day, leaving their names, leaving their stories in the hopes their loved ones would find them. The Rememberer might look weird, but she never forgot a name, never let a story slip through the cracks.

Suddenly the woman stiffened. Her face relaxed into a jowly mass of fleshy putty.

"Oooh yeah!" she cried without warning. "The Rememberer knows them. She lived with three bears in a little bower in the treetops. The boy too, he wondered where the birds sleep at night. The father was a man crucified upside down beneath the Golden Arches. They were given shelter by the Weasal named Pop. Say 'good-night,' Gracie."

The Rememberer went back to staring sightlessly at the screen. Drool streamed down the corners of her mouth as she began rocking back and forth again.

Phoenix grabbed the cabbie by the collar of his shiny blue king-fu jacket. He hoisted Bush Doctor into the air and stuck his face up against his.

"She's a psychopath, you little scumbag," he hissed. "You better have an explanation for this shit parade and it better be fucking poetry."

"L-lemme down," pleaded the cabbie. "Lemme down and I'll give it to you by the numbers."

Trench dropped Bush Doctor into a pile of concrete rubble, disturbing a nest of giant water bugs. The cabbie yelped as the enormous roaches swarmed over him, and jumped up, brushing insects off his body and out of his hair while he screamed in disgust.

DeLaCour used the buttstock of his M60 machine gun to smash the Checker's rear windshield to gritty powder, just for emphasis.

Raven cranked a round into the chamber of her Ingram MAC-10 and pointed it at the cabbie's nose.

"You got exactly one minute to make us believers,

guy," growled Phoenix. "Firty-nine seconds and counting . . ."

Words were gushing out of the cabbie's mouth in a nonstop stream. He was explaining so fast that he couldn't get them out slow enough to make any sense. Phoenix had to slow the dude down some before the cabbie was talking English again.

"Just checking you out to see who you were," the scared-witless cabbie finally managed to get out when he slowed down enough to make some sense. "These days you can't be too sure."

"What the hell are you talking about?" asked Phoenix. "Sure about what?"

Bush Doctor spread his hands.

"Look," he said. "Bush Doctor just a go-between, okay? People pay me to do odd jobs. In this case, I'm delivering a message to a man named Trench." He reached into his jacket pocket and whipped out an envelope.

Phoenix took it. Inside the envelope was a sheet of paper. Within the paper was a lock of blonde hair. Trench shook with rage as he held the hair between his fingers. A photo was enclosed. It showed his wife and son. Their faces were blank--zombie faces. By the pale gray bodysuits of the Dark Messiah's elite which they wore and those blank expressions, Phoenix knew the photo had been taken recently. Trench held the slip of paper beneath his eyes and began reading.

This time it's really them, Phung Hoang. No illusions. No special effects. We have them. Even if you don't believe the photo, you'll believe the hair. Whether they live or die is in your hands. Go to the river. Look across at Lady Liberty. Send up a single red Very flare. You will be helo'd to base.

The letter was signed: *Tallon.*

So John Tallon, the Butcher of Quang Tre, was still alive. Phoenix had thought him dead in the nuked embers which were all that remained of SCORF's Presidio hardbase in San Francisco after Phoenix had exterminated that nest of human maggots with a subkiloton nuclear device.

He had believed the Dark Messiah's right-hand man had been cremated in the Presidio firestorm.

Now Phoenix understood.

He, DeLaCour, and Raven had been expected. The crash through the Lincoln Tunnel had been monitored by SCORF. It would have had to have been. Tallon had been watching all the time. Orchestrating events. His perverted psychopath's mind coldly plotting their deaths.

You like putting things in boxes, don't you? Trench had once asked the merc honcho in Frisco. Now, he realized, Tallon had put them in a box of another sort.

Death awaited them when the merc decided to tear the box open. Tallon thrived on death. Phoenix had cheated Enoch's sadistic merc enforcer one time too many. In San Francisco it had gone beyond the merc's duty to his Dark Messiah.

It had become a personal contest between two sworn and bitter adversaries, two veterans of the Vietnam killzone whose battle extended into the twilight Endtimes of the almost-extinct human race.

"Okay now," said Bush Doctor, who abruptly turned to leave. "I be seeing you good people around. Take care." The cabbie walked smack into DeLaCour.

"Whoever you are, little man," rasped Phoenix, "you just stepped into something that's going to give you a whole new perspective." DeLaCour grabbed the guy and shoved him toward the parked Checker.

"Hey, m'man," the Cabbie said. "You can't be thinking about busting into Liberty Base. That'd be suicide."

Phoenix flashed Bush Doctor an evil smile.

"Watch me."

Part 2:

Buy the Maggots Lunch

8

Luxor.

A name out of the distant past. Priests' city where the dead were prepared for their voyage to the afterlife.

Here. Now. Lower Manhattan, from Fourteenth Street to Battery Park. Reclaimed.

For the Chosen. The Chosen of the Dark Messiah.

See them:

Faces blank. Eyes burning with a fanatic brilliance. Bodies straight, tall, held proudly erect.

Souls warped.

Brains dead.

Thoughts scrambled.

Children of the Dark Messiah, they had been hustled down into nuke-proofed bunkers buried deep within the earth's bowels just before the nuclear confrontation which turned the world into a cosmic cinder.

They had come from across the United States to join what others had called a "cult." But they knew better. They knew that what they were hearing from their prophet's lips were the unmistakable words of holy truth.

Here is what their Dark Messiah told them:

He told them that the Lord had willed mankind to undergo a terrible Tribulation. That the nuclear End-times were fast approaching.

This the Lord had spoken to him in drug-induced

visions of the terminal cataclysm which would sweep away the America in which they lived and replace it with a new, savage continent where only those who were strong would survive.

He told them that in these days and years of the nuclear Tribulation, mankind would sink to the basest, most savage depths of its long and violent history.

Man would be reduced to a state lower than that of wild animals. Men would drink each others' blood and devour each others' hearts. They would become bestial primitives in a second stone age from which they would never again emerge into the dawn of civilization.

He told them that this was the great cleansing by nuclear hellfire which the Lord had decreed to him in the visions of the future which he had beamed into his mind.

He told them that when this Tribulation had come to an end, the Dark Messiah's chosen would re-emerge into a world gone insane. Then and only then would the Lord's true work commence.

From the shattered rubble of pre-nuclear American society, the Dark Messiah's mindslaves would erect great cities in which the New Order would live. They would prepare for a new millennium in which they would be the unrivaled masters of the earth.

Now.

Here.

They would begin the great building.

Luxor.

Egyptian city of gods on earth. City of the Dark Messiah's mind-controlled children of chaos, his humanoid robot clones programmed to obey without question.

See them:

Human ants. Clothed in pale gray jumpsuits bearing the swastika of interlocking sevens that was the Dark Messiah's holy sign, they controlled earth movers to bulldoze vast stretches of bombed-out territory. Others hunched over the plans of bizarre new buildings, directing workers who climbed the metal superstructures rising from the nuclear garbage dump of the annihilated city. Swarming. Like . . .

Human ants.

One day soon, a strange and wonderful new metropolis, gleaming beneath a swollen red sun-blob, would stand here. Monorails would shuttle the Chosen to their jobs. Together they would march lockstepped to a common goal in total harmony, in perfect synchronization. There would be no crime, no strife, no emotion. There only would be order. *New Order.*

Human ants.

The Dark Messiah watched them busily at work. Screens deep below the earth showed him the hive creatures acting with a mass consciousness never before seen on the face of the earth. Each screen flashed him a new and different scene.

Here a mindslave, there a mindslave, everywhere a mindslave. Luther Enoch was pleased. His plans for Luxor were proceeding smoothly. Progress was being made.

Dark Messiah had a farm, ee-i, ee-i, oh.

Inside the high-carbon-steel biosurvival suit, what had once been the body of Luther Enoch was a putrid, semi-liquid mush of farting fluids. Plague virus swarmed through the organic death-stew, slowly killing the man imprisoned by a miracle of high technology. The man who had orchestrated nuclear Apocalypse had himself been destroyed by the joker in the deck.

Soviet Plague.

The incredibly virulent Russkie bugs had penetrated even the multimillion dollar filtration system of Enoch's private bunker, infecting even him as it spread like wildfire across the length and breadth of the United States turning millions into Contams.

The rapid mutations which Plague induced in its victims turned them into grotesquely disfigured giants. Growth regions in the brainstem went completely haywire.

Muscle tissue expanded as the bones stretched and grew, producing abnormal physical strength and massive warping of the skull and limbs. Fangs and claws replaced teeth and nails. The flesh grew to a thick hide, tough and leathery. In many cases Contams showed abnormal development of the sex organs.

At the same time, the brain atrophied down to only the most primitive core. Idiocy possessed the mind, while a constant sexual hunger tormented the crazed beasts. The bloodthirsty ghouls became violent before the growth process suddenly reversed itself in the Plague's terminal stage and the Contams slowly decomposed into puddles of slime.

In its early stages, organ transplants could stave off the progress of the Contam Plague disease. Millions from the Urban Containment Zones of nuked America had been rounded up like cattle and slaughtered like squealing hogs to provide the Dark Messiah's Chosen with a constant supply of fresh human organs to replace their diseased innards.

Others were stored in hundreds of specially constructed freezers across CONUS, freezers as big as football stadiums, the carcasses which they contained supplying spare body parts on a case-by-case basis.

Only one hope existed for the Dark Messiah: Alpha antibodies. They might arrest the disease's progress, maybe even reverse it entirely. But there lay the rub: Only one known source for the antibodies existed.

The Man called . . .

Phoenix.

Although Luther Enoch could never have known it, Phoenix's and the Dark Messiah's lives had become interwoven from the moment the nukes had detonated. It had turned out that way due to a million-to-one coincidence. Either that or what the Indians called bad karma.

An electronic tone suddenly sounded in the Dark Messiah's ear. Tallon had arrived at Luther Enoch's underground bunker. At Enoch's signal, his merc enforcer strode into the command-and-control room beneath Luxor.

John Tallon was in his customary field dress. Camo fatigues covered his body.

Across his chest, in a pit holster slung from a leather Sam Browne belt, was the vintage World War Two Mauser machine pistol the mercmaster carried, its grip inscribed with the twin lightning flashes and the grinning death's-head of the Nazi SS corps.

"We've made contact with Phoenix," Tallon told his master, getting down to business in his usual brusque manner. "Trench has received our message."

"Will he go for the bait?" the Dark Messiah asked, his voice pulsing in a chilling electronic monotone from the grille in the robot-man's black metal face mask.

"He's trapped," Tallon returned, a maniacal gleam in his cold gray eyes. "He has no other choice. By this time tomorrow, we'll have him. I promise."

"You had better be right, Tallon," said the electronic voice of Luther Enoch. "If not, the only other thing you'll be is dead."

Moonlight glinted on the gunmetal waters of the Hudson River.

Across the landscape of desolation, nothing moved, except the hunched and furtive animal scavengers of the night. Fires flickered in the distance, their lights dancing across the wasteland of microwaved Manhattan.

Headlight beams picked out a jittering path as the sound of a car engine grew louder. The Checker slid through the rubble-strewn streets, pulling to a halt at the water's edge.

Two figures climbed out of the cab.

Bush Doctor stretched his arms behind his back and took a long, deep breath.

"Ahhhh," he said, exhaling slowly. "Smells just like a blood-stained tampon, don't it?"

The grim-faced man standing beside him said nothing, but stared across the river at Liberty Island. The statue stood with her right arm held high. The torch it clutched, though, was dark.

Powerful searchlight beams crisscrossed the water, shining in the two men's faces as they went through their sweeps. More lights illuminated the concrete retaining wall that encircled the SCORF hardbase.

"Let's get it on," the cabbie said.

The grim-faced warrior raised his arm and triggered the Very pistol. There was a sharp report, and a second later a bright red flare hung in the sky, staining the river a blood-colored red as it drifted down again, leaving behind a faint wisp of gray-white smoke.

The helo's thuk-a-thuk came a moment later as a Cobra attack copter veered from the recon run over Lower Manhattan and banked sharply toward the position of the flare.

The crew swept the dockside with the helo's searchlight.

The halogen beam danced over the mounds of wreckage before picking out the two figures below.

"Stay where you are and drop your weapons!" the amplified voice called down from the helo's loudhailer. When the crew saw the warrior drop the M60 he carried to the ground, the copter made a cautious descent to the LZ, setting down with a lurch on its skids and a cloud of swirling dust.

Pointing a SCORF-issue Steyr MP169 SMG at the two targets, the copilot scrambled from the rotorcraft.

"He comes with us, you stay," said the merc to the cabbie.

"Sure thing, babe," replied Bush Doctor. "I just drive 'em where they want to go. What they do after that ain't none of my business."

Bush Doctor watched the Cobra lift off from the LZ. It hovered overhead for a moment, then with a slight sideward lurch, swung across the river with its nose down and pointing toward Liberty Island.

Minutes later, the Cobra was picked out by searchlights playing across its underbelly from the action stations on the Liberty hardbase. Securing priority clearance for landing, the pilot expertly set the helo down at the center of the well-marked landing pad.

Ducking the rotorwash, the captive trudged at SMG-point across a stretch of wet asphalt that glistened beneath the halogen arc beams lining the interior of the wall.

Military vehicles moved busily through the compound and armed personnel went about their duties with the look of crack military troops. Liberty Island was abuzz with activity, 24 hours a day.

Accompanied by an armed contingent of SCORF troopers, John Tallon strode quickly across the wet tarmac toward the prisoner. Both men stopped, their eyes locking as they stopped face to face.

A perverted smile twisted Tallon's lips into a Mephistophelian leer.

"So we meet again, Phoenix," he said as the sudden wash of a searchlight beam played over the prisoner's face.

"So we meet again, Phoenix," the prisoner replied. *"So we meet again, Phoenix. So we mee—"*

The Mauser barked in Tallon's fist, whipped from its coiled holster with blinding speed.

The 9-mm parabellum rounds sheared away most of the prisoner's face, leaving behind a ragged hole through which the interior of the pulped brain matter shone for a moment before spurting out onto the wet tarmac.

The body crumpled forward, jerking spasmodically as Tallon pumped three more rounds into its heart before reholstering the weapon.

Tallon turned and stalked away as his mercs dragged

the bloodied corpse to the disposal facility on Liberty Island.

Somebody would buy the maggots lunch for sending him a ringer!

9

A Hush-Puppy-silenced .380 quickburst made the two SCORF mercs dance like puppets jerked by unseen strings. The Hush Puppy silencer had been developed in Nam, mostly for shooting Viet Cong guard dogs, which is how it had gotten its name.

Gaping red holes, each spurting a stream of bloody gore, appeared across the fronts of the guards' paramilitary fatigues.

Guard One threw up his arms, did a half twist, and sprawled beside the HUMVEE they had been riding on their patrol of the Liberty Island perimeter wall.

The first kill's pard survived long enough to take three staggering steps toward the HUMVEE's cab, where another fragburst blew most of his head right through the windshield. Veins in its neck stump spurting blood, the corpse flopped to the blacktop flailing its arms and kicking its legs.

Phoenix slung the Uzi over his shoulder and signed to DeLaCour and Raven to break from the position of concealment just beyond the perimeter wall where the swift currents of the East River broke against the rocky shores of Liberty Island.

They had used those dangerous currents to float silently on the waters, bouyed up by makeshift pontoon floats they'd rigged from empty oil drums they'd welded airtight, until they came within landing distance of shore.

At that point, Phoenix and company swam for the island. Scuttling over the island's rocky beachhead, they had been dealt an unexpected run of luck as they saw a SCORF patrol car pull to a stop only a few score yards from their position and the driver get out, stretch, pull down his fly, and take a leak.

The second trooper had gotten out and lit up a cigaret, dragging deep while he looked up at the crescent moon riding on a few scudding clouds over microwaved Manhattan.

Boredom did that to soldiers. Made them careless. Put stars in their eyes. In the present case, boredom would also put bullets in their hearts. Careless men were easy targets, starry-eyed or otherwise.

Threading the Hush Puppy onto the Uzi's muzzle and flipping the select-fire lever to full-auto, Phoenix had broken for cover and killed both guards with a series of three clean noise-suppressed bursts. The first burst had kayoed Guard One. It had taken the next two to put the other guy away.

Now the assault team would scale the wall.

While Raven covered her two male pards, Phoenix and DeLaCour threw up lines tied to grappling hooks which had each been wrapped with three turns of electrical tape to muffle the sound of contact.

Both grapnels clawed onto the inside wall edge on the first throw, and Phoenix and DeLaCour tugged hard on the lines, testing them to make sure they were secure.

Satisfied, DeLaCour and Raven each climbed up the two lines while Phoenix covered their butts with the silenced SMG.

When they were over the top, he returned the Uzi to its breakaway rig on his thigh and walked up the side of the 30-foot wall with his legs crouched and the rope tight in his fists.

DeLaCour was already pulling in his line as Phoenix made it over the wall. Phoenix did the same, and he and

DeLaCour buried the lines near where they'd made their penetration of the SCORF Liberty Base compound.

If they needed to use the lines again on the way out, Phoenix and his crew knew just where to find them. Regardless of whether they got out the same way they'd come in, the lines wouldn't be easily discovered.

The trio found themselves in the shadows behind a huge cinderblock garage. They could hear military trucks inside the structure, the motors revving and swirls of exhaust smoke drifting through the cracked-open casement windows. Between the sounds of the revving engines, snatches of conversation came through too.

A group of SCORF cowboys suddenly rounded a corner. They headed for a squat building with a sloping roof. Hitting a button on the side of a metal door, they tramped inside.

"Not much happening topside," DeLaCour whispered. "Most of the facility must be underground."

"That's been the pattern everywhere else," Phoenix agreed. "Just like maggots to bury themselves in the ground."

"How do we get in?" Raven asked.

Phoenix thought he knew. Signing to Raven and DeLaCour to follow his head, he led them through the shadowy perimeter of the Liberty Island base, mindful of sensors that might be hidden to detect intruders, until he found what he was looking for.

It was a ventilation shaftway leading from the surface down into the heart of the underground complex. Through the metal grating covering the shaftway's opening came the muffled roar of throbbing machinery somewhere deep below ground.

The duct would lead down into the heart of the underground complex.

It would connect with a maze of branching shaftways which would give them access to every part of the base.

While DeLaCour and Raven covered him, Phoenix inspected the grating. It was secured to the frame by welded bolts. That meant the grating would have to be blown in order for them to enter the shaftway.

Reaching into the musette bag on his waist, Phoenix produced a claylike brick of C-4 plastic explosive wrapped in plastic.

He tore off a small hunk and replaced the rest in the military pouch.

Squatting beside the vent, he carefully tore off an even smaller hunk and rubbed it between his palms until it had been reduced to a thread of plastic HE compound roughly a foot in length.

Phoenix repeated the procedure until he had produced four identical threads of C-4.

Then he gently pressed the threads so that they formed a box around each corner of the rectangular grating. He then clamped two alligator clips firmly onto the grille, red and black wires corkscrewing from them to a miniature radio-controlled detonator and a battery pack.

The clips would conduct an electrical pulse from the battery pack when the receiver got the signal from the remote radio unit which Phoenix held.

Nodding to DeLaCour and Raven to take cover, Phoenix triggered the unit.

The long, slender, shaped charges of C-4 blew the grate with a bare minimum of sound. Though making little more than a muffled pop, the explosion was powerful enough to splinter the metal like matchwood.

Phoenix pulled the grating free and slid it carefully to one side of the opening to the ventilation shaftway.

"Virgins first," he said.

Tallon strode into the utility elevator, his jaw set, his eyes staring hard as the door closed.

He would need to reassess the situation. Think things through. He had a nagging feeling that Phoenix was on the base right now.

But he didn't want to put out an alert. He had fucked up too many times. He was facing a deep, black abyss and knew that one more misstep could provoke Luther Enoch into throwing him into the bottomless pit.

Tallon needed to think, he needed to cleanse his mind, unchain his soul.

The whore sat up on the bed as the merc entered the room. She saw the hard cast to his face. She knew what he wanted of her.

She was at once afraid of and aroused by this man, knowing what he was capable of doing to her body and her mind.

"I want it," Tallon barked. "Now." His eyes took in the large round breasts that were barely covered by the flimsy black negligee. He could see the woman's nipples harden under his gaze, tightening with fear and sexual hunger.

As she rose to her knees, Tallon ripped the negligee from her body. Her heavy breasts gleamed beneath the light, their nipples now fully erect. Without a word, she took his already rigid organ into her mouth and felt it throb and swell to even greater size and thickness.

Tallon pulled his cock from her mouth and placed it between her breasts. He wanted to see the jizzum splatter her face and make her gasp as it got into her nose.

"No," he husked. "*This way . . .*"

Light grew at the end of the darkened shaftway. It had started out as a pinprick in the total blackness as he had belly-crawled through the ventilation shaft, and had slowly, yet steadily irised to a full circle of brilliance.

Phoenix crawled to the grating at the end of the metal duct and looked out through the grillwork of intersecting iron bars. He was looking down into a cavernous room full of throbbing machinery which filled the vast enclosure with an earsplitting turbine wail.

An iron catwalk just below the air vent, some ten feet from the ceiling, encircled the dynamo room. Phoenix lay stock still for a full five minutes, until he was convinced that no workmen or other personnel were inside the room.

Digging the steel toes of his boots into one of the riveted cleats in the airshaft for leverage, Phoenix punched the grating cover out of its frame, and heard it tumble to the metal scaffolding with a clatter that was almost completely muffled by the loud, continuous throbbing from the machinery below.

Followed by DeLaCour and Raven, Phoenix crawled out of the shaftway and onto the catwalk. Since the ventilation duct which they had been following from the surface dead-ended here, they would have to find another route through the rest of the underground complex.

"Where to now?" asked Raven.

Phoenix looked around, considering their position and weighing their options.

Metal stairways positioned at each crook of the rectangular catwalk descended down to the cavernous room's lower level. A single firedoor was set into the wall of the section of catwalk directly across from the one on which they stood, probably leading to a storage area. Immense metal conduits—some hissing steam while others sweated beads of condensation—which hung from metal supports snaked across the ceiling and around the walls.

Machinery bulked below, emitting a high-pitched turbine wail as it pumped life support throughout the underground complex.

"We've gone down only two levels," Phoenix said. He remembered the SCORF underground complex he'd penetrated at the Presidio in San Francisco, and reasoned it was even money that this base was constructed according to a similar architectural plan. The generator room would form the heart of the complex, with the labs, maintenance bays, administrative offices, and living quarters radiating outward from it in concentric circles.

"Doesn't look like there's a hell of a lot of choice,"

continued Phoenix. "It's either back the way we came or down one of those access stairs."

DeLaCour and Raven nodded their agreement.

The Liberty base penetration crew moved stealthily down the stairway.

"Freeze or burn! It's your call!"

Phoenix whirled. A merc hit man was scrabbling for the SMG holstered at his hip. In the pulsebeat that had passed from the sound of the merc's voice, the guy had succeeded in getting the subgun half out of its holster.

Before he could fist the weapon, the noise-suppressed Uzi in Trench's hand spoke, launching a whispering burst of .380-caliber retribution at the scum soldier which stitched the guy across the throat, ripping away his larynx in a messy hunk.

The merc dropped the weapon and flopped forward like a windup toy with a busted mainspring. He tumbled off the catwalk with a scream that was cut short as the guy did a swan dive straight into the rotating steel blades of a mammoth cooling fan which were moving at a blur. The fan made an ugly grinding sound and blood fountained from it as it sliced the merc to grated sleaze in only a second or two.

More mercs came running.

DeLaCour swore loudly, glancing up the way they'd come. By now the commando backup was pouring out onto the catwalk, deadly heat belching in their fists as slugs sang and sparked against the deck and sides of the metal parapet.

No way to get back the way they'd come.

The only way was through the generator room.

Phoenix unleashed another noise-suppressed .380 caliber burst from the Uzi, firing from the hip. A merc went down, his arms and legs kicking out as the body thrashed in a terminal swim stroke. Right behind the dead man, another merc was getting set to pitch an M34 FRAG grenade at the three intruders.

The merc was cut down before the grenade left his hand. The blast blew him and the three soldiers around him over the railing of the parapet, scattering body parts all across the enormous generator room below. Jammed by foreign objects, the machines began to smoke and sputter and give off a sickening stench that was a combination of burning flesh and smoldering wires.

DeLaCour fired blind around a corner as more SCORF hardguys were pouring onto the parapet.

Catching sight of a stretch of pipe leaking steam that was between his crew and the troopers, Phoenix unleased a burst which ruptured the pipe. Boiling-hot steam spilled out in scalding clouds of jetting vapor. SCORF hit-paraders screamed in agony as they were boiled like lobsters where they stood.

The mists of the ruptured pipeline also obscured the strike crew's fast sprint down one of the metal access stairways and across the generator room to the corridor beyond.

The corridor was bare and lit by overhead fluorescents. Signs along its length bore arrows which pointed toward various sections of the subterranean complex.

GENERATOR ROOM

LOADING BAYS

BARRACKS

COMMAND AND COMMUNICATIONS

OFFICERS CLUB

Sprinting through the corridor, the strike crew suddenly found all passage blocked by a contingent of SCORF mercs which materialized from around an L-shaped bend.

"Move!" Phoenix hollered, spraying the troopers from the hip with .380-caliber poison, while DeLaCour and Raven took off back down the corridor toward the generator room.

As the mercs sucked floor, Phoenix pitched a smoke grenade, pivoted, and beelined it after his pards.

He ran straight into a brick wall.

A wall of mercs which had cut off the other end of the corridor.

Pinned between the two SCORF kill crews, Phoenix was a sitting duck.

John Tallon stepped through the camo-suited ranks.

The merc honcho smiled.

This time there was no way out.

Phoenix was caught like a fly in a pisspot and Tallon had his fist tight on the outhouse chain.

10

"Armageddon must agree with you," Tallon told Phoenix. "You're looking good, Phung Hoang."

Phoenix was held in shackles. Surrounded by a contingent of armed SCORF troops, he was being force-marched at SMG-point into a large-capacity utility elevator that was shuttling them topside.

DeLaCour and Raven had vanished. Only they knew where.

"I knew you wouldn't be able to resist my invitation," Tallon continued. The other two intruders weren't important. Let them escape, Tallon thought. He'd hit the jackpot and that was all that mattered.

"This was all needless, you know," Tallon went on as they rode up to the surface level of the Liberty Island hardbase. "I told you that I wanted to deal. You could have walked in here without any opposition. I'm a man of my word."

"I know what you are," Trench returned. "You've not even a man."

Tallon's face hardened. A muscle twitched beneath his right ear. For a moment it looked as if he would whip out his Mauser and start blasting. The merc got himself under control, though, as the moment passed. He forced a smile.

"You're not going to rain on my parade, Phung

Hoang," Tallon told Trench. "I've got you and you have zero options." Tallon smiled again. "You thought we'd have your wife and kid locked up below ground, didn't you? You were wrong."

They reached the top level of the Liberty Island hardbase. Phoenix was silent as the door slid open and they exited onto the rain-slick tarmac of the SCORF compound. Tallon pointed upwards.

"They're in there," he said.

The statue. Inside Lady Liberty's head, 30 stories above the surface of the island, Sandra and Brian Trench were held prisoner. It was like something out of a medieval legend.

A helo was on the landing pad, its rotors a circle of speed blurs as it prepared to lift off on a patrol run across the Manhattan Urban Containment Zone. Military transports rolled across the wide expanse, lumbering through the gates in the concrete security wall like prehistoric leviathans.

Searchlights played out across the river.

Tallon's men marched Trench at weapons-point across the tarmac toward the entrance to the Statue of Liberty in the mammoth stone pedestal on which she stood. Troopers in visored crash helmets and Kevlar body armor stood guard at the statue's base. They packed full-auto M16A2 rifles and Ingram MAC-11 SMGs as sidearms.

Suddenly, out of the corner of his eye, Trench caught a flicker of movement.

Without turning his head, he focused in on the section of shadow near the wall from where the movement had come, instinctively knowing that it had been a signal from Raven and DeLaCour.

Phoenix tensed for action.

Their play would come any second. He had no idea what form it would take, so he braced himself for anything, tensing the muscles in his legs to lash out at the ground nearest him whenever the play went down.

BLAMM!

The explosion came directly in front of him as DeLaCour flung an APERS grenade at the mass of troops.

Phoenix lashed out with a side kick, striking the guard to his side in the hip and driving a jagged wedge of bone through the guy's bladder. The guard's legs buckled underneath him and he went down vomiting blood. As he did, Phoenix grabbed the Ruger AC-556 assault weapon from the commando's limp fingers.

Full-auto heat blazed from Raven's fist as she launched lead at the contingent of guards from the other side, cutting down three mercs as they dipped for their hand cannons.

"The chopper!" DeLaCour yelled.

Phoenix saw Tallon reaching for the Mauser holstered across his chest. Tallon was just behind him, regaining his cool after a split instant of shock and reacting with deadly speed.

Slashing the Ruger's stock in a vicious arc as he whirled to the left with his weight behind the swing, Phoenix rammed the side of the weapon against Tallon's jaw. The merc spat teeth and fell backwards, bowling over two SCORF cowboys who were at that moment bringing their Ingram SMGs into blasting position.

Phoenix used the diversion to cover his end run toward the Apache chopper. DeLaCour and Raven already were a few dozen feet from the cockpit, as the flyboys were preparing to lift off the landing pad and begin their patrol.

Seeing what was going down, the pilot revved the rotors faster, trying to gain altitute before the uninvited passengers with the chattering cannons climbed aboard. The flyboy in the seat beside the pilot unslung an M16A2 short-barreled rifle from an overhead rig and opened right up with a 5.56-mm autoburst that was his way of saying "no visitors welcome."

The burst hit the tarmac a few yards shy of where

Raven had dropped to one knee and was bringing a compact yet deadly Uzi .45-ACP-caliber SMG into firing position. She didn't intend for the helo's side-gunner to live long enough to get off another burst.

As the flyboy swung the 5.56-mm blaster for a second try, Raven stitched the cockpit with a quickburst of lethal steel which shattered the plexiglass with an ugly splintering noise and punched the top of the shooter's skull right through the back of his neck.

The guy flopped sideways, doing a barrel roll as his momentum tore open the cockpit door and he hit the ground with his shoulders while his legs were still tangled up inside the cockpit. As the chopper lifted a few inches off the rain-slick tarmac, the pilot managed to boot his former partner the rest of the way out the door. The corpse did a half roll, then the bloody puppet lay spraddled in eternal rest.

Another autoburst sheared away most of the pilot's lower jaw and tore a raw hunk out of his chest cavity, which splattered the instrument panel with blood and bits of bone and organs. Moments later, DeLaCour reached the Cobra's cockpit and pitched the dead flyboy out the door.

Raven climbed in the other side, firing over her shoulder as she took cover behind the Apache's armored door, ricocheting bullet fragments shrieking all around her as the merc crew opened up with everything they had.

"Come on!" she yelled, seeing Phoenix zigzagging in a broken-field run to avoid a hail of SCORF lead as he made the last few yards toward the copter. DeLaCour, at the controls, was holding it ready for takeoff with one hand on the joystick and the other fisting a steel-spitting Uzi SMG.

A line of punctures suddenly perforated the blacktop between Phoenix and the chopper. Phoenix stopped short and whirled to face the attack.

A HUMVEE was rolling fast across the tarmac, the

M60 MG mounted on its roof kicking out a razoring hailstorm of death at Phoenix as he sprinted toward the helo.

WHAM! WHAM! WHAM!

Mortar strikes sent incinerating toadstools of fire erupting from the ground, effectively isolating Phoenix from the Apache, encircling the running man in a cordon of jackhammering steel and cremating fire.

No go.

He was cut off.

"Get out of here!" Phoenix screamed at DeLaCour, and began emptying the Ruger's 5.56 clip at the fast-moving HUMVEE. "Move it!"

The HUMMER went up in a fireball as a longburst from the Ruger pierced its fuel tank, scattering flaming steel and burning body parts across the compound.

DeLaCour stared at Raven. Both suddenly realized there was no way Trench would be able to reach the helo in time. If they waited any longer they would all be taken.

Phoenix watched as the helo lifted off the pad. Almost instantly, a line of yellow 7.62 tracer rounds punched upwards from the machine-gun emplacements on the Liberty Island perimeter wall.

The metalstorm missed the copter's underbelly, sailing up into the blackness. For a few seconds, it looked as though the helo would get out of range of the SCORF guns.

Then a burst caught it just aft of the cockpit.

"Goddamn it, no!" Phoenix screamed. "No!"

A fireball blossomed from the stricken helo's rear. The fuselage cracked in two, one half spinning out over the dark waters of the East River, the other half crashing against the jagged rocks surrounding Liberty Island.

Searchlights played jerkily across the river and the island's rocky shoreline. Nothing alive moved. Only debris floated on the surface of the water.

Phoenix fell to his knees and smashed his fists against the blacktop until his hands were bloody and raw, not believing that his friends were gone.

A heavily armed squad surrounded him and he was taken prisoner all over again.

The base of Lady Liberty housed administrative offices for the SCORF hardbase. Medical facilities were located there too.

Phoenix sat on a steel examination table in a medical ward separated from the rest of the unit by hospital-room partitions on heavy casters. A doctor was bandaging his shoulder where a bullet fragment had furrowed the flesh.

"You're lucky the fragment ricocheted off the bone," the doctor said, holding an X-ray negative up to the ceiling lights to examine it after he was finished. "If your shoulder bone hadn't been there to stop it, there's no telling how much damage it would have done."

Phoenix stared at the sawbones but didn't answer. His mind was elsewhere: under the oily black waters of the East River where DeLaCour and Raven were probably feeding the fish by now. The medico turned and walked away.

"How's the patient doing?"

The doctor shrugged as John Tallon entered the heavily guarded ward, blocking the doctor's path. "Physically, there's nothing wrong with him. Psychologically, you've got a seriously burned-out individual there."

"War is hell, Doc," Tallon told the doctor with a smirk. "And in hell you burn." The doctor left the ward. He didn't have time to bullshit. There was work to do. The firefight had left him with dozens of seriously wounded men who needed patching up in a bad way.

Tallon found Phoenix sitting on the examination table. The merc took out a pack of cigarets—vintage pre-war Marlboros, not the synthetic shit the government handed out nowadays—and lit up, tasting the rich smoke on the back of his tongue. The cigs had come from a plundered warehouse in Montana, and were worth as much as rare wine had been before the war.

"I should kill you, Phung Hoang," he began, exhaling the creamy smoke. "If the choice was mine alone, that's just what I would do." Tallon pulled the Mauser from its pit holster and, leveling the barrel at Trench's head, cocked the hammer. "Putting a bullet through your fucking head would be the best thing for all concerned."

Tallon put away the Mauser. "But the choice isn't mine," he went on. "My orders come from the man who runs this country now, and he says you live. For now, anyway."

"Until they operate, you mean," Phoenix returned. "So Luther Enoch can crawl back out of the slime. It won't make him a human being, though. Enoch was always slime."

Tallon was enjoying the game. He'd been waiting a long time to confront the man before him now. He was toying with him like a cat toys with a mouse. He relished what he was about to say next.

"There's another way to do it, Phung Hoang," he said. "One that won't involve killing you."

Tallon told Phoenix about The Child.

A mutant being born to the warlord of nuke-blitzed Brooklyn, The Child was the only known source, beside Magnus Trench himself, of the Alpha-Immune antibodies which could treat Soviet Plague. It was known that The Child had wiped Plague virus from the bodies of thousands in the year since he was born.

Phoenix was no longer necessary as long as the Dark Messiah had The Child. There were enough Alpha antibodies contained in the mutant's system to produce enough serum to cure the Dark Messiah's elite of Plague.

"You lead us to The Child," Tallon said. "Your wife and son are free to go. We'll even arrange transport to the Western Nuke-Free Zones," Tallon went on. "Wish I had travel brochures, Phung Hoang. There are trees and mountains and lakes there. It's just like it was before the war. An earthly paradise, and it's yours. In return for The Child."

Tallon paused to let his words sink in, watching the look in Phoenix's eyes as he absorbed what the Dark Messiah's merc honcho had just told him.

"Where are they, butcher?" Phoenix returned. "Show them to me."

Tallon smiled. He had been waiting a long time for this moment.

"Your wife and son are right here, Phung Hoang," he answered. "Safe in the statue's head. They have a room with a view—if your idea of a view is a lot of garbage, that is."

With catlike quickness, Phoenix had the collar of Tallon's tunic bunched in his fists. The smile faded from the merc's lips as the clicking of automatic weapons primed for blasting came from the troopers positioned all around them.

"Better let me go," Tallon rasped. "Or I won't vouch for what happens next. To a lot of these guys filling both of us with holes would just mean a promotion."

Phoenix released his grip on Tallon. "Take me to them," Phoenix said. "Now."

Tallon was only too glad to oblige. Surrounded by a crew of heavily armed men, the merc honcho took Trench up to the top of the Statue in the service elevator. There they stood outside a steel security door flanked by two armed troopers.

"They're waiting for you, Phung Hoang," Tallon told Phoenix. "Right behind that door." The merc turned the handle and pushed open the door. Phoenix could hear the sound of breathing from inside. But it was strange breathing.

He walked into the room.

What he saw turned his blood to ice water.

His wife and son were in hospital beds. Their bodies were swaddled in cocoons of life-support machinery which kept their conditions stable.

Phoenix knelt between the two beds, stretching his arms to cover the bodies of the two most precious things in his life. Then he couldn't hold the tears back a moment longer and silently wept.

11

The Apache chopper hovered over the LZ for a few seconds after the warrior who had just jumped onto the trashed streets of Manhattan moved at a fast, loping trot into the slanting rays of the setting sun.

The flyboys satisfied that their end of the mission was in the bag, the chopper shot straight up to an elevation of 30 feet, banked sharply over the mounds of rubble, and arced off toward Liberty Island.

Both men in the chopper were relieved once they'd cleared Manhattan and were out over the choppy waters of the East River.

Flying over the mass graveyard where over eight million bodies had been incinerated in the holocaust which had consumed Manhattan made them nervous.

Although their macho code prevented them from admitting it, each man felt like a little kid who'd climbed into a cemetery at midnight on a dare. Each felt surrounded by the presence of millions of ghosts pointing skeletal fingers at them in mute accusation.

Phoenix felt no guilt as he heard the thuk-a-thuk of the Apache's rotors fade into a faint drone and the helo disappeared into a deepening twilight. He was a ghost himself, his life stolen from him on the day of nuclear Armageddon.

Instead, as the ripple soles of his high lace-up boots

crunched over the debris-littered streets of the crucified city, the wan light of the dying sun glittering off shards of broken glass projecting from the heaps of wreckage which dotted the trashed landscape, Phoenix felt oddly at home.

Midtown. Sixth Avenue and Forty-ninth Street. The heart of the city's Diamond District.

Impossible to believe that this zone of total devastation had once been one of the most bustling areas of New York, the broad avenue filled with buses and cabs, huge skyscrapers lining it on either side for 20 blocks creating the effect of a manmade canyon, street hustlers, monte players, and Chinese guys with lo mein carts doing a steady business with the crowds thronging the sidewalks.

Phoenix tried to pick out landmarks which he could plug into his memories of the heart of Midtown in order to recreate the place in his mind, but the holocaust visited by the 20-megaton citybuster of a Soviet nuke had been so complete that there was little left to remind him of the past.

The fire-scorched and soot-blackened girders which jutted from the slag heaps like immense burnt matchsticks told him nothing about the skyscrapers which had once stood there.

Here at ground zero, the devastation was nearly total, and only his compass showed him the way toward the lower end of the island.

By now it was five o'clock in the afternoon and daylight was fading fast.

Chances were it would be the last daylight Trench would see for a long time to come. Although his destination was the Wall Street area of Lower Manhattan, from which he would somehow have to get across the East River to Brooklyn, the SCORF Apache had taken him as far as it could.

Anywhere beyond Manhattan was off-limits to the chopper.

The badass army led by Abraxas was in total control

of the borough of Brooklyn. Odds were that the crew would be fired on and the helo blown to hell before Phoenix even touched ground.

And Brooklyn—specifically Abraxas's home base at Coney Island—was to be Phoenix's final destination. From here until there, he'd have to go it solo.

Although the Manhattan Bridge alone had survived the nuke strike partially intact, it was now a no-man's land, its Manhattan side controlled by SCORF, its Brooklyn end in the hands of Abraxas's badass warriors. Trying to cross it alone would have been tantamount to suicide.

Phoenix knew that his only shot at crossing the East River separating Manhattan from Brooklyn lay in using the IRT subway tubes which still ran beneath it.

Although flooded by the nuke blasts and too damaged to be reliably used for subway traffic, the tunnels were still intact and largely drained of water.

Allowed to arm himself from the SCORF Liberty Base arsenal, Trench had chosen weaponry and survival equipment which would be especially useful along the route he had decided to take into the Brooklyn warlord's turf.

Slung across his chest, riding crosswise on a breakaway rig attached to a chest bandolier, Phoenix carried a Beretta M3P 12-gauge autoshotgun.

The fully automatic weapon was a cross between an SMG and a pumpgun, and could unload its ten-round clip of 00 lead with the speed of a trigger pull. Since each shotgun round was the equivalent of nine .32-caliber bullets, a burst of the thunder-stick could vaporize any living thing that moved.

That kind of firepower would be a life-saving asset if Phoenix ran up against the mutant life forms called Contams on his crossing of the river.

From past experience, Magnus Trench was painfully aware that the flash-mutated products of Soviet Plague virus had a natural affinity for tunnels and underground installations of any kind.

They bred in the dark, fetid places like subway

tunnels, and Phoenix fully expected to find nests of the slime beings in the grisly hustle which lay ahead.

Strapped to Phoenix's right thigh was an Ingram .380 MAC 11 submachine gun. The "Mini" MAC was no bigger than a conventional handgun, yet could crank out withering autofire at a cycling rate of better than 900 rounds per minute.

It was also accurate when set in select-fire mode, and controllable enough to be fired without using its retractable buttstock. The MAC had been a dependable ally on Phoenix's trip through hell so far, and he was confident that the weapon wouldn't let him down this time either.

An M16A2/M203 over-and-under combo completed his armament package.

The full-auto rifle was fed by a 32-round clip of 5.56-mm hollowpoints, while the under-mounted 40-mm grenade-launcher was capable of launching FRAG or APERS mortar rounds at a pull of the trigger.

Plenty of ammo was available with a fast grab from pouches on military webbing around his belt, as well as M34 FRAG grenades slung from the eyelets of his chest bandolier, armed for detonation at a pull which would disengage the cotter pins which held their spoons in place.

Rations and a compact first-aid kit had been brought along too.

As always, his Vietnam-War-issue K-BAR survival knife was kept within close reach, this time strapped to his left ankle where he could whip it from its oiled leather scabbard with one swift movement.

Perfectly balanced, the K-BAR was ideal for throwing as well as for stabbing an enemy at close range, and when its nine-inch tempered-steel blade sliced through a vital area, it was deadlier than any bullet.

Maybe the most important piece of gear Phoenix carried was the ANVIS night-seeing goggles, which were kept in an olive drab pouch to one side of the M3P autoshotgun.

The sophisticated electronic light-amplification system would allow Phoenix to see clearly in total darkness by amplifying even the tiniest photons of light to the point where images could be naturally discerned.

Even in pitch blackness, visibility could be as good as in broad daylight as soon as the ANVIS system was put on line.

Aside from a few Manhattan scavs, scurrying through the nuclear hellscape of the blown-to-shit borough and scattering at the weapon-laden doomsman's approach, Phoenix didn't encounter any problems as he trudged southward toward the entrance to the City Hall tunnels through which he would make the crossing beneath the East River.

A pack of six stray dogs soon latched onto him, though, yapping close at his heels throughout most of his trek through the trash heap of urban civilization.

But the canine hangers-on didn't make any attempt to harm him, and Phoenix allowed the leg-lifters to accompany him while he walked. He figured they had latched onto him out of curiosity, or looking for a handout, or out of an age-old instinct in their breed dating back to the time of prehistoric man to seek out human companionship.

Less than two hours after hitting the Diamond District LZ, Phoenix arrived at his destination, the City Hall subway station near what had once been the seat of New York City Government.

The area's brick buildings, most of which dated back to the turn of the century, had been knocked flat by the nukes and only rubble remained. The office buildings on Park Row, however, still stood partially intact, although they were all leaning against one another like a row of tumbled dominoes.

Standing on the shattered concrete base that had once been a statue, but which was now a mass of molten slag in a flat area that had once been City Hall Park, Trench looked east toward Brooklyn, along the smashed wreckage of the Brooklyn Bridge.

The Brooklyn half of the bridge was partially submerged in the river, while the Manhattan half had been completely vaporized by the blasts of N-Day.

Phoenix scouted out the area, noting that the entrance to the station was blocked by debris, but knowing that the subway tunnels which ran beneath could be reached through one of the ventilation casements located along their length. He spotted one nearby, and decided to use it as a way of getting down into the tunnel.

While the pack of yapping dogs sniffed the ground at his feet, Phoenix sat on a heap of rubble and broke out some of his rations.

Before heading down into the subway tunnel he threw the leg-lifters some of the food.

While the dog pack fought over the scraps, he got up and quickly disappeared below the ruptured sidewalks of Nuked York.

Bush Doctor's mouth was set in a broad smirk as he peered through a pair of binoculars from his position behind a wall of the upper story of one of the smashed buildings along Park Row.

Monitoring the SCORF transmissions had paid off. He had picked up signals which had given him a pretty good idea about what was happening.

He'd watched traffic patterns in and out of Liberty Base and spotted the SCORF Apache setting down.

With his uncanny knowledge of the ripped-apart streets, Bush Doctor had driven to a point near the LZ and scouted the area on foot.

He'd seen Phoenix disembark and kept his distance as the heavily armed man made his way toward Lower Manhattan.

Replacing his field glasses, Bush Doctor climbed back down to street level and got back in Li'l Stinky. The cabbie knew where Phoenix was heading: He was heading into Brooklyn.

Into the turf of the warlord called Abraxas.

Bush Doctor knew when he had information worth selling. More importantly, he knew where the information he now had would prove valuable.

12

Duckwalking along the gently sloping corridor which opened on the mezzanine level of the subway station, Phoenix carried the M16A2 assault weapon in point-and-shoot position in his right hand, while in his left he held a sealed-beam flashlight which lit the way ahead.

At the mezzanine area at the corridor's end, a token booth fronted a row of turnstiles, beyond which a short flight of stairs gave access to the subway platform below. A wrought-iron gate which stretched from floor to ceiling at either side of the row of turnstiles partitioned off the mezzanine from the platform.

Playing the flashlight beam in a wide arc across the subway station, Phoenix scoped out the area, alert for any signs of hostile presence. Seeing nothing to alarm him, Phoenix slung the 5.56-mm chattergun over his shoulder and vaulted the turnstiles in a fluid leap.

He would use the ANVIS goggles when he penetrated deeper into the tunnelworld, he decided.

For now, he would rely on the powerful halogen flash he carried to cut through the murk.

Graffiti-covered walls leapt to life as the brilliant flash beam played over them, and Phoenix felt the way he had when he had visited the Lascaux caves in Southern France years before and seen the primitive paintings prehistoric man had left behind on the walls.

The flash beam also picked out far more gruesome artifacts of the vanished civilization of pre-nuclear America.

Two pairs of eyes gleamed suddenly from a newsstand on the platform, its racks still lined with moldering copies of porno magazines, and Trench saw the nauseating apparition of two enormous rats gnawing the bones of one of the two skeletons which dangled out of the news kiosk.

These were apparently a new mean breed of super-rat. Unlike pre-war rodents, these rats didn't scurry into the shadows. Instead, they hissed at the living human, baring vicious yellow fangs as they readied themselves to spring.

A .380 MAC burst reduced the belligerent rodent scavengers to so many dollops of glop, which splattered the faded ad posters on the tiled walls with rat puree. Reholstering the compact Ingram SMG, Phoenix crossed in front of the newsstand before continuing past it down the platform's length.

Nearby, two skeletons were frozen for eternity beneath a section of wall which had collapsed and pinned them under tons of concrete rubble. Bits of their clothing were still attached to them. Insects had nested inside the skulls and crawled in and out of the empty eye sockets of the fleshless remains.

Cautiously moving on booted feet down the fissured concrete surface of the station's platform, Phoenix saw hundreds more bodies scattered all around in this post-nuclear Pompeii.

Some had been completely stripped of clothing and flesh by scavengers and the forces of decay, while others had become mineralized by the action of water dripping through the layers of concrete above and turned into human fossils. Laden with salt and other minerals, the waters seeping through the flesh and internal organs had literally turned the corpses to stone.

The air stank of death and decay, and the spoor of the verminous grave robbers was everywhere.

Human scavengers had also visited the mass grave. The skeletons and mummies had been stripped. Many had their pockets turned out, and articles of every description littered the platform.

An IRT express train had been pulling out of the station when a searing EMP pulse generated by a Soviet nukeburst miles above the doomed metropolis burned out its electrical system, stopping it dead.

The last car of the derelict subway train was still inside the station while the remaining nine cars were hidden within the tunnel.

Mummy faces, grotesque in death, were pressed against the doors and windows of the final car in a jumbled heap.

The IRT car's front door had been forced open and skeletons were lying in piles on the pavement where hundreds of passengers crushed each other in their wild stampede toward the rear of the train to escape the deathtrap which the express had unexpectedly become.

It was fortunate for Phoenix that the express had been heading uptown instead of downtown, in the direction of Brooklyn. If it had, the blocked tunnel would have meant leaving the station and searching for another method of getting across the river.

Holding the M16 "Shorty" in his right hand and the halogen flash in his left, Phoenix jumped onto the railroad bed and crossed onto the southbound tracks.

Suddenly, the tunnel exploded with the sound of shrieking and the frenzied slapping of leathery wings.

Phoenix ducked as thousands of bats which had been roosting in the roof of the abandoned subway station swirled around in panic, having been disturbed by the only human intruder in many months. He took cover until the swarm had quieted down and again returned to their roosting places on the ceiling of the cavernous subway stop.

Crossing the tracks, he shone the halogen beam into the tunnel, relieved that it was free of obstructions and noting that a layer of sucking mud covered the tracks, deposited by the flooding of the subway system on the day the nukes had detonated.

Setting the flash down on the concrete surface of the subway platform and pointing it upward for maximum illumination, Phoenix took out the ANVIS goggles and slipped them over his head, adjusting the elastic strap which held them in place for comfort and tightness.

Flicking on the ANVIS unit, he ran through a quick status check, assuring himself that the goggles functioned properly.

Then, flicking off the halogen beam and stowing the lantern in a military pouch, Phoenix began cautiously moving into the subway tunnel, walking along the tracks, the snout of his weapon ready to blow anything that challenged him straight to hell.

The masked figure strode across the rubble strewn landscape like a spectral king of the dead. The low-income housing projects which bordered the Coney Island amusement park and which were Abraxas's destination had been spared by the blasts of nuclear Armageddon.

Either the Soviet warplanners had not bothered to target the area, or the guidance system of the warhead meant to destroy the zone went off course.

Or then again, it might have been the hand of a capricious deity given to practical jokes on a cosmic scale.

Whatever was responsible, the city projects survived. There were 20 high-rise towers, each jutting 60 stories into the air, which now dominated the skyline as the tallest buildings in the hellblasted city of Nuked York.

Before the nuclear holocaust, the low-income projects had housed families on welfare. Street gangs had carved up the turf of Coney Island into private fiefdoms. Junkie hookers strolled the mean streets of one of the city's sleaziest ghetto areas. Arson turned vacant apartments into shooting galleries and crack dens.

At night the projects echoed with the sound of

screams and the staccato report of automatic-weapons fire as the rival gangs battled it out for control of the profitable drug trade and prostitution traffic in the neighborhood.

By some perverse irony, the nuclear holocaust which had reduced the rest of the Big Apple to a radioactive slag heap had left the asphalt jungle of Coney Island virtually unscathed. While the cream of society rotted in their grotesque mass graves, the most violent and vicious segment had been allowed to survive.

Abraxas was aware of this irony more than anyone else. He had once been the law in the area. His name then didn't matter. His occupation had.

Abraxas had been top cop on these mean streets. He had once been the captain of the 60th Precinct, which some had dubbed "Little Vietnam" because of the open warfare conducted on its streets.

He had been a guy who had come down hard on the drug dealers and the pimps and the shooters who infested the asphalt jungle and turned it into the cesspool it was.

But the nuke blast had changed all that. In the aftermath of the holocaust something in the mind of Abraxas had snapped.

He could remember N-Day as clearly now as the moment the horror had dawned on a new and savage age.

He had seen the World Trade Towers vaporized by the Soviet airburst. All the phone lines suddenly went dead. Even the emergency radio link with Brooklyn Borough Command was silent.

The rule of law had been replaced by the rule of terror. Abraxas had exchanged his NYPD blue for biker-badass black leather.

Those members of his command who refused to obey were publicly executed, their tongues torn out with red-hot pincers, their noses, ears, and cocks hacked off, and their headless bodies strung up on girders of the elevated tracks of the Brighton Line subway. Most, however, fell into place.

There was a ready-made kingdom to be ruled over. Thousands of scum people from the city projects were awaiting iron-handed leadership. Abraxas provided that leadership. His only price was total obedience.

Moving swiftly, Abraxas eliminated the rule of the gangs with a savagery which surprised even the denizens of the tough turf of the ghetto. The mutilated corpses of those who wouldn't capitulate had hung from the lampposts for the birds to pick clean as grim reminders that Abraxas would not tolerate being fucked with.

His power consolidated, Abraxas had next forged the thousands under his command into a deadly fighting force. The badass army marched across the nuked borough of Brooklyn, effortlessly overwhelming the gangs which challenged them, putting their leaders to death and absorbing their forces.

In no time at all, Abraxas ruled over the entire borough as a warlord feared by all, yet revered by many as a power which had prevented their lapse into a state of total chaos.

Then came The Child.

The Child which gave him the greatest power of all.

The power to heal.

Through The Child he had the power to give life as well as take it. Through The Child the diseased were cured of their terminal afflictions. Through The Child Abraxas held absolute power over those he ruled.

And The Child had given him another gift. The gift of *seeing*. With it, Abraxas had the power to look through The Child's eyes, through the mutant's brain, and know the unknowable.

It was like watching a television screen showing the future and the past.

Through The Child Abraxas had been given the eyes of omnipotence. And the seeing existed for him alone. No one else had been able to see through The Child's eyes.

No one except Abraxas.

The wind from the sea whipped across the warlord's face as he climbed onto his motorcycle and revved its engine, his badass flunkies falling into line behind him.

Together they screamed off along Surf Avenue, past the amusement park that was now a place of trial by fire.

Abraxas rode hard and rode far. He gritted his teeth. His men knew better than to ask questions.

Their leader had just come from a Seeing.

What they did not know, what they could not know, was that Abraxas had just seen his own death through the eyes of The Child.

13

Coming to a point where the subway tracks he'd been following began to slope gently upward, Phoenix realized that he was nearing the midpoint of his journey.

Scores of feet overhead flowed the waters of the East River. His journey had taken him half the distance across the subway tunnel's length. It had not been completely straight, though.

Far from it.

The tunnels formed a Gordian knot of passageways snaking and burrowing through the bedrock of the city. Navigating by compass and keeping to a due westerly course, Phoenix had made several detours since going down into the City Hall station two days before.

In some cases, stalled subway trains in the middle of tunnels had forced him to crawl through maintenance passages and the narrow conduits which housed sewer lines and electrical cables in order to reach a point beyond the trains blocking his path.

At other times, the tunnel he was in began to follow a course that took him in a different direction entirely from the one he wanted to go in.

Moving cautiously, he holed up during breaks in service bays, located deep within the network of tunnels, which were used by maintainence crews inspecting tracks or making regular repairs to the subway system.

Apart from more oversized rats and a swarm of giant mutant roaches which glowed in the dark due to a high radioactivity level, Phoenix had encountered no other form of life.

The tunnels were silent, the silence broken only by the scurrying feet of four-legged scavengers and the steady dripping of water percolating down through layers of bedrock from the river above.

Phoenix found the subway system remarkably intact, and that contradicted his experiences elsewhere in the nuked United States.

San Francisco's BART transit network, for example, had spawned an army of Contams. The ghouls had burrowed down into the cool, damp tunnelworld from which they emerged to feed when night fell.

The underground tramway which ran beneath St. Louis had been infested with Contams too.

Phoenix and his Omega Force companions had fought a pitched battle on more than one occasion with mutant foragers on their mission to penetrate the SCORF concentration camp beneath the Spirit of St. Louis arch.

And the underground nuclear-missile launch complex through which Phoenix had struggled after escaping from the madwoman who ran Earthwomb near the desert shiekdom of Las Vegas, although not designed for passenger traffic, nevertheless followed the pattern of underground passageways.

Here in New York, though, the tunnelworld through which Phoenix moved seemed to be the exception to the rule. Animal scavengers notwithstanding, the subway network seemed to be mutant-free.

The explanation, of course, might be that the New York subway system was so extensive that the relatively small section of it through which Phoenix had passed didn't represent the entire system. The rest could be Contam Valhalla for all Phoenix knew.

Checking his compass to ensure that he was proceeding on course, Phoenix began scouting for a place to set down. Through the light-amplifying ANVIS goggles, he saw that the tunnel was opening up to yet another deserted platform.

If it checked out, he would camp here for awhile before beginning the final leg of his journey.

Fisting the short-barreled M16A2, Phoenix padded silently on booted feet across the last few hundred yards of track lying between himself and the mouth of the tunnel. As he reached the tunnel mouth, he cautiously reconnoitered the station ahead.

Water damage had destroyed most of the turn-of-the-century tilework which covered its walls. Huge stalagmites and stalactites had grown from floor to ceiling across its length. A narrow concrete platform divided the Manhattan-bound local track from the Manhattan bound express track. A similar platform divided the Brooklyn-bound local and express tracks.

On the express track, Phoenix saw a train twice as long as the normal ten-car subway train.

Except for the skeletonized human remains of a single person at the front of the train, Phoenix could detect no human presence.

Jumping onto the platform, Phoenix cautiously approached the skeleton. Very little was left of the striped motorman's uniform draped loosely around the gnawed bones, but there was enough to tell the story.

Phoenix quickly realized that he had come to a parking area for subway trains stored during off-peak periods.

From here, trains could be routed during rush-hour traffic to make up for shortfalls in service. The absence of human remains confirmed that this station could not have been used by normal commuter traffic.

Deciding it was safe enough to switch from the ANVIS goggles to the halogen arc lantern, Phoenix removed the flash from the pouch and flipped it on.

He walked along the platform toward one of the cars of the parked train, which had its three doors open instead of fully closed, as were doors on the rest of the train.

Before going inside, he checked out the entire train. Satisfying himself that it was clean, he went into the car he'd picked out and sat down on one of the blue formica benches which ran lengthwise along the car.

The lantern, placed on its end on the dirty salmon-colored Masonite floor, gave him enough light to see by. Eating some more of his rations, which he washed down with water from his canteen, Phoenix stretched out on the bench seat with his hand on the butt of the M16A2.

Next thing he knew, one of the dogs which had befriended him days before was running toward him. Phoenix reached into his pack, but instead of rations pulled out his .380 Ingram . . . .

Phoenix awoke with a start. Sounds, ghastly scraping sounds, echoed in his mind. His heart was jack-hammering in his chest and a cold film of sweat coated his body.

The lantern, Jesus God, where was the lantern!

Darkness closed around him like a clinging wet sheet. Choking darkness. Reflexively he checked his Huer. The chronometer's glowing face told him that he'd been asleep for four hours. Anything could have happened. Four hours down in this underground hell could be a lifetime.

Again the sound came!

Phoenix scrabbled for the ANVIS goggles hanging around his neck. Sliding them into position around his face and switching them on, the suffocating darkness was instantly replaced by a flickering green electronic light.

The subway car's interior was empty. The lantern was gone, though. Whipping the full-auto M16A2 into defense position, Phoenix jumped from his seat and raced onto the platform.

Death waited there for him.

Its red eyes glowing in the darkness, the first Contam leapt from atop the subway car's roof, its jaws open to reveal a row of hooked sickles poised for tearing away the victim's throat.

Sidestepping the leprous ghoul's death lunge, Phoenix sent a burst of 5.56-mm whizzers into the rotting Plague mutant's abscess-covered midsection.

The hollowpoints exploded as they entered the putrid, slime-dripping mass, splattering the subway car with fetid-smelling gore. A second burst completely obliterated the shambling monstrosity's disfigured head. Blood spurted in thick gouts from the corpse's neck stump as the Contam collapsed inside the subway car.

More Contams were spilling out of an enormous rupture in the subway wall which Phoenix had failed to notice when he'd entered the station. Some of the Contams wielded crude clubs, their blunt ends ringed with metal spikes.

Others brandished makeshift axes, swords, and other lethal cutlery made out of wickedly honed steel debris, which in their hands made for deadly bloodletters.

Most of the Contams, however, were unarmed. But all the weapons they really needed were contained in their immensely powerful muscles, their razor-sharp fangs, their hooked claws on hands and feet, and their lust for human blood.

Slinging the M16 Shorty over his shoulder, Phoenix hoisted the M3P autoshotgun. It was the weapon he had chosen for use against Contams in the tunnels of the Nuked York subway system. Its wide fan of 00 shot practically guaranteed a hit, and the automatic cycling of 12-gauge cartridges meant that it was capable of doing devasting damage.

Phoenix aimed the bullpup-configured M3P at the center of the mass of slobbering mutant scum freaks which were advancing on him, moving remarkably fast for creatures as large and heavy as they were.

A burst of 00 shot reduced the gibbering cannibal slime beast at the point of the charge to bloody hamburger. Parts of blown-away organs twisted as they fell in a splattering nova all around the destroyed underground denizens.

Phoenix triggered another 12-gauge deathburst, destroying all the remaining Contams rushing him.

But they were only the beginning.

Contams were now pouring by the dozens into the subway station. They were now more than making up for the absence of mutant ghouls prior to attack. It looked like every Contam in the Nuked Apple was closing in for the kill.

Phoenix ejected the spent clip from the M3P and palmed a fresh ten-round magazine of shotgun shells into the weapon. Holding it in his left hand, he whipped the MAC-11 SMG from its hip holster and fisted it in his right.

Jumping from the platform onto the empty Manhattan-bound express tracks, Phoenix cut loose with the two full-auto weapons. Twin lances of flaming death blazed and blitzed in his triggering fists, wiping out the Contams as they closed in for a crude kill.

Phoenix wasn't kidding himself, though. There was no way in hell that he would be able to singlehandedly take out a swarm of ghouls this size.

It was by far the largest concentration of the Plague-infected mutants he had seen in his journey through the hell of post-nuclear America.

He didn't have all that many options, though. The options boiled down to three: either stand and fight, try to head back the way he'd come, or hustle toward Brooklyn and hope to outrun the Contam kill crew.

Since the first two options were a joke, Phoenix had no choice but to tear ass for the tunnel in front of him, firing behind him as he ran.

But the Contams were in the tunnel too. They slowed him down so that the main attack force of mutants had enough time to pile into the tunnel. Needing to make a fast getaway, Phoenix released two grenades and pitched them overhand.

Bad move.

The trackbed shuddered. The force of the explosions weakened the already badly stressed and blast-damaged concrete. Millions of cubic tons of river water above made the fissures widen. In minutes, the water was pouring in, a raging flood. As Phoenix ran further along the tunnel, a vast section of tunnel roof gave way with a thundering crash and fell to the tracks.

Kept out for generations, the East River flooded the subway tunnels like an angry giant. The surging, sluicing currents roared in Phoenix's ears as the concrete of the tunnel collapsed with a stomach-turning groan and the rumble of the speeding tide of death grew louder until it was all he could hear.

Looking behind him, Phoenix saw a wall of water filling the circular passageway behind him, sweeping up the Contams as though they were insects caught up in a flooding ditch.

In another moment Phoenix knew that he would be going for a long, hard swim.

14

Phoenix looked around for anything he could grab onto against the bone-crushing onslaught of the wall of water that was coming at him at the speed of a runaway express train.

The concrete walls of the narrow tunnel which curved upward on either side to an arched roof were smooth, but in this type of tunnel there was a narrow concrete retaining wall at hip level which provided about a foot of clearance between the sides of the tracks for subway workmen to stand on when trains passed.

An electrical power conduit, sheathed in metal insulation which was painted a bright yellow, ran the length of either side of the tunnel. At intervals of six feet, bare lightbulbs stuck out of the conduit in wire mesh cages.

The IRT tunnels were the oldest in the subway system. Not only were they too narrow for the faster, newer trains, but they hadn't originally been wired for electric lighting. The newer tunnels of the IND and BMT lines were wider and had been wired with internal power cables.

This combination of factors probably saved Phoenix's skin. The narrowness of the older IRT tunnel in which he was stuck meant that the flood of East River water took seconds longer to flow through it, giving him critical reaction time that he wouldn't have had elsewhere in the subway system.

The external electrical conduits which ran along the walls gave Phoenix something to hold onto while he braced himself against the onrushing tide of death. If he'd been in one of the newer tunnels of the system there would have only been smooth, blank wall on either side, with nothing to grab hold of.

Hands locked onto the projecting power conduit and his feet hooked beneath a narrow iron railing which ran along the outside of the retaining wall, Phoenix hung on for dear life and held his breath as the wall of liquid death washed over him with a deafening roar that was like the scream of a wounded hell beast.

Doing better than sixty miles per hour, the wall of water coursed through the narrow tunnel with enough velocity to have bowled him over, drowned him within seconds, and carried his corpse away like the bodies of the dead Contams which bumped Phoenix as the flood sped them through the tunnel.

As it was, the force of the madly racing water was so enormous that it almost ripped away the power lines and the railing to which Phoenix desperately clung, and practically dislocated his arms and legs from their sockets as it hammered viciously at the human body caught in its path.

Minutes after the first rush, though, the ferocity of the flood had abated somewhat. The flood had practically filled the tunnel, leveling off just below Phoenix's Adam's apple. His lungs near the point of bursting, Phoenix shook the water out of his face and gasped for air.

Although the air was rank with decay and smelled as foul as a septic tank, it was now as sweet to Phoenix as a bouquet of roses. Phoenix allowed his painfully throbbing arms to relax a little and sucked as much air as he could get into his lungs, listening to his oxygen-starved heart hammer in his chest.

All that he'd been granted, he knew, was a short reprieve. Sure, the flood's fury had stopped as the tunnels filled and the pressure of the river above equalized with that of the flooded passageways underground, but it didn't take a construction engineer to realize that the foot or two worth of air pocket that lay between his head and the ceiling of the IRT tunnel wouldn't last more than a few short minutes.

Already Phoenix could see the water level begin to rise. A few moments ago it was at Adam's-apple height. Now it was up to the dimple in his chin. Five more minutes, max, and it would be game-over time for Magnus Trench.

Up ahead, there was a service entrance in the tunnel wall which either led up to the street level or an underground room which might hold any number of things, from spare parts for electrical equipment—or might just be for trackworkers to hole up in during their long shifts underground.

Although Phoenix couldn't see the service entrance now, he was sure he had spotted it just before the liquid shitstorm hit. Feeling the water beginning to tickle the bottom of his nose, Phoenix began crawling along the wall toward the service entrance as fast as he could.

It seemed like it took forever to reach it, even though the arched doorway in the tunnel wall couldn't have been more than three, maybe four, yards away from where Phoenix was. Because it had a flight of concrete stairs angling up into the roof of the tunnel, the water level was only up to the lowest few steps of the flight. The rest of the way up was clear.

Hustling up the flight of stairs, Phoenix found himself in a narrow concrete bunker about ten feet above the flooded IRT tunnel.

More breathing room, okay, but still no more than a temporary reprieve.

The water filling the tunnel from which he'd just escaped was already climbing the stairs and pouring into the room. In a couple minutes more the room would be totally submerged and Phoenix would still be yesterday's news.

Phoenix desperately cast about for a way out, expecting to find nothing. The room measured roughly ten feet by twenty, the walls made out of cinderblocks held together with cement and covered by a thick layer of paint.

It was empty except for a few large wooden spools that had once contained coils of electrical cable.

As the water level increased, the bouyant spools began to float and swirl around as the pressure created a miniature whirlpool in the room.

Swept up by the whirlpool, Phoenix hung onto one of the immense wooden spools as though it were a life preserver.

The pressure of the water was pushing him steadily toward the concrete bunker's ceiling. There was only about five feet left before the room was completely submerged.

Then Phoenix saw it.

Near the ceiling, set in one of the bunker's walls, there was a metal hatch which he guessed led to a maintenance duct for one of the electrical conduits which had relayed power to the miles of subway track.

A heavy padlock secured the hatch, which looked like it would otherwise easily open.

Aiming the MAC-11, which he hoped still worked despite being submerged for long minutes beneath the surface of the rising water, Phoenix aimed at the lock and triggered a .380 burst.

The MAC performed beautifully, firing an eight-round burst without jamming once. And the burst was accurate. The lock splintered as the hardnose rounds penetrated its iron casing. As the eddying current brought him close enough, Phoenix grabbed for the padlock and threw it from the latches it secured.

The heavy iron door swung open into a crawlspace which was barely large enough for a man to squeeze through. It was either do just that, though, or sprout gills.

Phoenix wriggled into the crawlspace, just ahead of the fast-rising water level, thankful that there was a latch on the inner side of the metal hatchway which he could hold shut with the toe of his boot while the water level filled the room.

The enormous pressure of the water beyond the crawlspace was enough in itself to keep the hatch sealed tightly behind him.

For the first few moments after he'd entered the crawlspace, Magnus Trench just lay there, all energy drained from his body, wishing he was dead.

Sometimes the horror overwhelmed you. No matter how you adjusted, no matter how many times you'd survived, the horror waited to take over.

This was one of those times.

Magnus Trench had felt the horror many times in the Vietnam hellzone. He had felt it on long-range patrols into the heart of enemy territory like a suffocating madness that seemed to close in around him like a second skin.

It had happened to others. It was part of the psychology of battle fatigue. And Magnus Trench had known then, as he knew now, that if it was allowed to take possession of the mind, a soldier was as good as dead.

Because war, the war in Nam and the war in postnuke America—all war—was at root insane. It turned the soldier's world inside out. It placed those who fought it into situations which tested their will to survive to the utmost.

Those who refused to adapt to the madness died.

Phoenix breathed deeply, shutting his eyes, sucking dank, putrid air into his lungs. He exhaled slowly, mentally going through a yoga relaxation routine until he was in control again.

When his heartbeat had slowed to near normal and his mind was clear again, he took stock of his situation.

As near as he could tell, he was at the mouth of an electrical maintenance crawlspace. The submerged concrete bunker he had just escaped had probably been used for storage of electrical equipment during periods of construction.

The crawlspace would have allowed a subway maintenance engineer to repair shorted cables and blown transformers.

Because it had housed high-voltage electrical equipment, the crawlspace was lined with ceramic insulation which made it waterproof—another factor which had probably saved Trench's life.

But Phoenix had no way of knowing how far the crawlspace would take him. There was every likelihood that it extended only a few score yards into the bowels of the subway system to where the cables branched off, in which case he would have only succeeded in buying himself a few more minutes of life.

Probably, though, the crawlspace led into another tunnel on another level of the system. Few subway tunnels in the city ran individually; they were usually bundled together on multiple levels serving several subway lines.

Yeah, Phoenix might conceivably find his way into another subway tunnel. But that subway tunnel might be underwater. In which case, Phoenix would still be one dead hombre.

There was only one way of finding out, though.

Move.

Phoenix had no choice but to do just that.

The crawlspace sloped gently upward, but followed a generally horizontal path. Phoenix quickly noticed how hot it was inside, but that was to be expected.

The heat was a product of the service tunnel's ceramic lining, and it was far better to drown in your own sweat than in a million gallons of river water, Phoenix had to admit.

The tunnel ended a hundred yards ahead, terminating in a metal hatchway identical to the one through which Phoenix had entered the crawlspace.

Crawling up toward the hatch, Phoenix held his ear to

the cold metal, listening for any sign of what was beyond it.

Several minutes later, he had heard nothing but a dim rushing sound which might have been caused by anything, including the East River rushing through the flooded tunnel beyond.

If that was the case, if and when Phoenix got the second hatchway open, he would be immediately drowned.

Listening having proven inconclusive, Phoenix felt around the edges of the hatchway. There was some seepage of moisture around the seal of the hatch, but again, it was not enough to tell him anything about his chances of finding a flooded tunnel beyond the door.

Phoenix lay still and considered his options. It didn't take much brainpower to realize that he'd run fresh out.

The tunnels through which he'd come were now permanently flooded by the East River. If the tunnel ahead of him—if in fact there was a tunnel there and not another crawlspace or a conduit too narrow for a man to pass through—was also flooded, then he would die.

Would die.

That would be it.

Die in a nameless grave beneath Nuked York City. One more of the nuclear war's millions upon millions of victims. And it would have all been for nothing.

For nothing.

Phoenix exhaled slowly.

One way or another, it looked like get-down time again.

Backing up down the length of the crawlspace, Phoenix unslung the M16A2 and got out a FRAG mortar round. Loading it into the M203 underbarrel launcher, he screamed as he triggered the can.

Nothing happened.

Phoenix cursed. The soaked mortar round had dudded out on him. He reached for another, repeating the process. With his luck they would all be damaged.

Ka-Blammmm!

The force of the dead-on mortar strike punched through the steel hatchway as though it were made of brittle plastic. Noxious smoke swirled back into the tunnel, propelled by inrushing currents of air from the tunnel beyond.

Coughing from the fumes despite having held his breath, Phoenix belly-crawled toward the open mouth of the conduit as fast as he could.

Stretching to the left and right as far as he could see was another subway tunnel. Phoenix scanned the roof for cracks, but apart from some superficial fissures, from which dripping stalactites jutted down to where they were met by upthrusting stalagmites, there was no major damage.

"*Damn!*" he whispered softly, dropping to the tracks, the single syllable as much of a cry of exultation as a curse and the only sound he permitted himself to make in the potentially deadly tunnel.

Checking his compass, Phoenix began walking the rest of the way toward the blitzed boro.

Book Two:
. . . Reap the Whirlwind

Thou must know, Sancho, that the valor which has not prudence for its basis is termed rashness and the successful exploits of the rash are rather to be ascribed to good fortune than to courage.

—Don Quixote

Part III:

The Lion, the Tin Man, the Scarecrow, and Dorothy

15

Clark Street—Brooklyn Heights, the decaying sign read.

It was the first station Phoenix had come upon since he'd crawled out of the electrical conduit hours earlier. From the sign at the subway stop, Phoenix knew where he was.

He was underneath the borough of Brooklyn.

A layer of putrid muck now covered Phoenix's body from head to foot. His sopping-wet boots squished with slime as he walked, and his camo fatigues were pasted to his body.

Although his nose had long before grown numb to the stench, Phoenix knew that he stank like a two-legged septic tank from the East River whirlpool bath he'd just had.

A grim smile cracked his features as he thought of all the chic assholes who had paid big bucks in Manhattan beauty salons to lie in huge troughs of mud like human earthworms, believing it would be good for their skin. He wondered what they'd say to the beauty treatment he'd just received. Morons like those superficial jerk-wads had blown away the world in a terminal nuclear orgasm.

They had beautified their flesh, yeah, but their souls—those had been left to fester and rot.

Up ahead, the concrete platform of the subway station stretched ahead of him. Aside from a few places in the cracked ceiling where water was slowly dripping, it was dry as they came.

Phoenix vaulted onto the platform. Checking his chronometer, which still functioned despite the beating it had taken, Phoenix noted that it was a few hours until daybreak on the street above.

Indeed, there was enough light spilling into the station from casement gratings high up in its vaulted ceiling to allow him to see without the use of the ANVIS goggles he'd worn throughout his trek through the tunnel.

Phoenix would rest here awhile, and while he rested, would decide whether he would continue deeper into the blitzed borough of Brooklyn by way of the subway system or streetside from the station he had now reached and go the rest of the distance above ground.

Before doing anything else, though, Phoenix knew that there were three things that couldn't be postponed.

The first thing was that he had to clean his weapons and check his ammo supply for water damage.

Second was that he'd have to dry out his clothes and get some of the muck off his body.

Thirdly, he'd have to get some chow into himself and grab some badly needed sack time.

From the lay of the land, Phoenix figured that his current position was reasonably secure. Scoping the place out, he hadn't detected any animal spoor, recent human leavings, or any other evidence that the place had been visited since the day the earth went bang.

When he moved, though, the odds said that shit would start to hit the fan. So Phoenix both needed and wanted to be as well prepared as possible.

Although there was enough light to see by, there wasn't nearly enough to go through a systems check the right way. Without his lantern, which he'd lost in the Contam attack, he'd have to risk lighting a fire.

There was no shortage of kindling available in the

station. Garbage of all kinds was strewn everywhere. Firewood was readily available from the wooden benches spaced along the platform.

Using the long, tempered steel blade of his K-BAR survival knife to hack through the long slats that made up the benches, Phoenix managed to assemble a respectably sized pile of firewood in only a few minutes of work.

A book of matches which had survived the dunking in a waterproof pouch lit the kindling—made up of a couple of cellophane Cheez Doodle, Deli Fries, and Tostitos bags, Mars Bar and Three Musketeers wrappers, and other debris scavenged from the platform floor.

The large capacity platform garbage can had yielded an unexpected treasure: Somebody had stuffed a bunch of corrugated cardboard cartons inside it. Phoenix sliced the cartons into strips and added them to the top of the woodpile.

Blowing gently on the flames until the woodpile caught, Phoenix soon had a nicely crackling fire going on the floor of the platform.

A chain slung between the banisters at the foot of a flight of stairs that led up to a bricked-up entranceway with a firedoor in its center had a sign on it that read: ENTRANCE PROHIBITED. The chained-off entrance was only a couple of feet from the bonfire Phoenix had made.

Shucking off his sopping-wet camos, Phoenix draped them over the chain, where they'd be in a perfect position for the fire's heat to dry them off.

Then, hauling the now-empty trash bin over to the edge of the fire and laying it on its side so he'd have something to rest his back against—as well as some cover to fire from in case any uninvited company arrived—Phoenix took out the deadly tools of his profession and laid his weaponry out in front of him.

The guns were dirty as a well-digger's asshole and their innards were gunked up with slime and mud from the crud bath they'd just had, but with a thorough cleaning they'd be as good as new.

Phoenix wasn't as sure about the ammo, though, and would have to count on more than his share of misfires when using it. He made a mental note to be extra careful about covering his ass when firing his cannons until he could get his hands on some fresh, reliable ammunition —which didn't appear to be anywhere in the near future right then.

Keeping the Ingram, which had remained fairly dry throughout the ordeal, close at hand, its stock loaded with a clip containing 32 125-grain roundnose slugs, Phoenix took down the M3P autoshotgun, cleaned it thoroughly, fed it a fresh magazine of ten 12-gauge shells, and repeated the process with the M16A2/M203 over-and-under assault weapon.

Soon the freshly cleaned and oiled weapons gleamed healthily on the concrete deck of the platform.

Phoenix used the fire to heat up a can of rations, which he held over the flames on the end of his K-BAR and ate silently, his eyes, ears, nose, and brain on full alert to the slightest hint of movement around him.

In Nam, taking a bath in the bush was almost like hanging a bullseye on your backside, and now, sitting buck naked in a concrete cave in the postnuclear jungle, Magnus Trench felt doubly vulnerable. He wolfed down the hot can of meatballs and spaghetti in two big mouthfuls, tipping back his head and dumping the can's contents into his mouth with one hand while the other clenched the stock of the MAC 11 SMG. Sack time was out: He was too wired to sleep.

By the time his clothes had fully dried, the amount of ambient light in the Clark Street station was enough for him to see normally by. His camos were warm as toast as he climbed into them, immediately feeling like less of a stationary target.

Phoenix chucked the empty rations tin onto the tracks and began quickly saddling up, stuffing the M3P into his breakaway rig across his chest and the Ingram .380

SMG into the holster on his thigh, while holding the short-barreled M16A2 assault weapon in the crook of his right arm.

Fed and rested, he felt better than he had in days. He was now ready to begin the final leg of his journey.

And, yeah, he didn't feel like messing with any more tunnels. Whatever the dangers to be encountered topside, Phoenix had taken his last subway ride for a long time.

A bird cawed somewhere in the distance as Phoenix cautiously exited the subway station onto the block-busted streets of Downtown Brooklyn. *Something* cawed, anyway. Who knew what the fuck it was.

Standing in the midst of another little Hiroshima that had once been the Nuked Apple's second largest business district—and the only one in the outer boroughs to rival Manhattan—Phoenix swept his glance over a panorama of urban devastation which was as bad as or worse than what he'd seen in the gutted ruins of the Midtown meltdown.

Choking and clogging the sidestreets which spread out from Flatbush Avenue onto which he had exited from the subway station, Phoenix saw hundreds of trashed automobiles piled up in a solid wall of twisted wreckage which rose to several stories.

The walls of many of the buildings on either side of the avenue had collapsed and fallen to the ground, exposing their interiors, which formed an ugly gridwork of empty boxes. In most cases the floors had given way and the tons of furnishings had spilled down to the ground floor level, where they now lay in rusted, useless heaps of wreckage laced with the skeletal remains of the buildings' human occupants which had fallen along with them.

Enormous craters, some of them large enough to swallow a small building, dotted the landscape where gas mains had exploded and erupted from beneath the earth like miniature volcanos. The front end of a city bus protruded from one of these craters, which had partially filled with a pool of mucky water through which the snout of something broke the surface as Phoenix looked into the pit.

Consulting his compass, Phoenix began following Flatbush Avenue, which he knew was the most direct route across the blitzed borough of Brooklyn.

He'd covered only a mile worth of ground when he found himself passing through the ruins of a shopping mall that had once had an A&S and a Mays department store on either side.

He heard the sounds of booted feet crunching concrete rubble first, then the faint though unmistakable click of a bolt action cocking a round into a weapon's firing chamber.

Spinning fast on his heels, Phoenix instantly brought the M16A2 into position, glad now that he'd taken the time and trouble to get his firearms into as good condition as he was able before hitting the mean streets of the blitzed borough.

Two badasses, both of them black and both wearing their hair in bright green Mohawks, were coming at Trench from atop a mound made up of the rusted shells of cars and buses. Both geeks were packing Uzi .45-caliber SMGs. Screaming and hollering like the fucking Indian braves they thought they were, the street trash had the biggest grins on their faces you ever saw as they leveled their full-auto weapons at the guy they were about to take off.

It had been their intention to light Phoenix up while his back was toward them, and one of the punk slimebags had already brought the Uzi into hip-shot position to do just that. Too bad for them that Phoenix had spun around before the chumps had time to jerk their triggers.

A split-second before Phoenix had completed his turn, the screaming, whooping badass braves each triggered a full-auto quickburst. The butterflies of .45-ACP lead kicked hell out of the rubble a few feet short of his new position, though, and Phoenix avoided getting hit. Shame on them.

It was a close shave, though. *Too* goddamn close a shave.

Before Badass One could whip the .45 ACP Uzi back into fly-and-die position, or his brother maggot get off a burst from his own heater, Phoenix unleashed a blazing 5.56-mm gut-ripper from the M16A2.

The burst caught Badass One high on the chest, stitching a diagonal line of ragged punctures from his left shoulder to lower jawline that changed him from vicious prick to Moby Dick as he spurted a dozen whale spouts of blood.

As death reflexes made the muscles twitch and jerk, the crude dude went into a terminal breakdance that ended when his legs kicked out from under him and he slid down the side of the mountainous pile of wreckage on his face, splattering his pard with intestinal guacamole.

Badass Two was lucky. He was stained with his scum brother's vein juice but otherwise unharmed. He was a fast little fucker too, street savvy as a mutant sewer rat and twice as ornery.

The shooter from scum had enough sense to drop back behind the pile of wreckage just as a FRAG can thundered from the M203 grenade-launcher and punched a huge, flame-belching fissure in the side of the mountain of scrap metal.

The next sound Phoenix heard was that of a motorcycle engine revving hard from behind the wreckage. An instant later, Badass Two was vrooming straight at him astride a Harley Davidson panhead which had been outfitted with some very deadly goodies.

A shield of scrap plate metal protected the scoot's front end, while its wheels were bulletproofed with additional armoring over their rims. A bizarre Viking helmet, painted silver and with two iron wings sticking out of either side, now covered the head of Badass Two, who fisted his Uzi as he popped a wheelie while clutching the ram's-horn-shaped handlebars with one hand.

As the badass goosed the cycle, pouring on the steam as he headed in a suicide charge at Phoenix, blistering .45-ACP firepower poured out of the Uzi he fisted in his other hand.

Phoenix dodged sideways, then down, just ahead of a line of bulletholes which kicked up dirt and debris at his booted feet. Just as the cycle-mounted badass was passing him, Phoenix pivoted and simultaneously brought the 5.56-mm assault weapon into target acquisition.

A line of autofire punched at the rear tire, but didn't connect as the cyclist skidded for a second pass, his SMG belching lead before he shot forward at 60 miles per hour, a song in his heart and a snarl on his lips.

Phoenix went down, tucked sideways under the line of fire, did a half roll onto his left shoulder, and popped back up like a lethal jack-in-the-box throwing blazing metal from a half crouch.

A lancet of 5.56-mm tumblers struck Badass Two square in the face, causing his head to explode like a popped balloon full of bright red puke.

As the headless hardman went flying to one side to crash into a pile of refuse, reverse momentum made the bike go spinning off in the opposite direction.

It skidded around in a looping circle before coming to a rest against a derelict garbage truck lying on its side.

Phoenix scrambled to his feet and sprinted across Flatbush Avenue toward the downed cycle. The wheels had stopped spinning as the engine automatically cut off. Righting the heavily armored Harley, Phoenix saddled up and stomped hard on the kick starter, pulling out the automatic choke.

Nothing happened.

Either the scoot had been damaged in the crash or it was just acting ornery. Phoenix tried kick-starting the recalcitrant hog a second time.

At first he thought he heard engine backfire, then

realized it was the sound of the badasses' pards coming at him fast and mean.

Turning his head, Phoenix saw a couple more scoots and a car that had been specially armored screaming around the corner.

"Start, goddamn you!"

The Harley roared to life on Trench's next try. All it had needed was a little cussing. Phoenix maxed the throttle and screamed ahead of the ratpack in hot pursuit, just as another crazed urban Injun leapt onto the rear of the Harley hollering and whooping and prepared to split Phoenix's head open like a bony melon with a meat cleaver only slightly smaller than a kitchen door.

To make matters worse, two armored crew vans pulled nose-to-nose directly ahead of the speeding getaway cycle as the panels in their sides slid back and gun barrels popped out.

In another few seconds, Phoenix was Alpo, one way or the other.

16

BRAT-A-TAT-A-BRAT-A-TAT-A-BRAT!

A banshee choir of bullets sang past Phoenix as he ticked off the seconds he had left to live before either catching a round in the bike's gas tank or slamming head-on into the sides of the armored vans. There was nothing Phoenix could use as a ramp to gain enough altitude to jump the bike over the roofs of the vans.

Besides biting the dust, there was only one option left. Phoenix grabbed for it like a junkie grabs at a dirty needle, hoping to get lucky, though not even half believing he would.

To his left gaped the ruptured wall of one of the department stores which had bracketed the downtown shopping mall. Whipping the fast-revving cycle hard to the left, Trench went into a skid that tucked his head a cunt-hair under a crossfire of badass lead, the cycle's wheels bumping over piles of garbage as he revved inside the wall.

Holding their fire, the badass kill crew watched the cycle vanish into the trashed interior of the department store and pulled up short. The leader of the shark pack, a tall muscular Puerto Rican with tattoos all over his face and a braided sidelock hanging from his cueball skull, in a pair of black leather chaps with cartridge bandoliers crisscrossing his naked chest, waved some of his twerp troops forward.

"Follow the maricone," hollered the crude dude, "bring that dogfucking Anglo come-wad to Falco!"

The badasses locked eyes, sharing the same unspoken thought. Nobody in or out of their right mind wanted to go in there. That was bushwhack city. Bullet gulch. To a man, each wanted to tell their fearless leader to go piss up a tree.

But they knew better than to give their bossman any backsass. Guys who, when told to jump, didn't ask how high, or when told to fart, didn't ask in what key, quickly found themself face down in their own guts with maggots instead of eyes.

More afraid of Falco than they were of the guy inside the wrecked A&S department store, the two Indians unslung their blasters and cautiously approached the big hole in the wall, their guns jerking back and forth like the wavering antennae of frightened shit-flies buzzing around a spider's web.

A graveyard grin spread across Phoenix's face as he hunkered in the shadows of the first-floor lobby behind a pile of shattered women's mannequins. He knew he had only seconds to shake his shit, but there was still enough time to make it shine.

Working quickly and silently, he propped one of the mannequins he'd pulled off the layer of garbage that covered the floor on the seat of the Harley and lashed it fast with a hunk of electrical wiring he'd yanked out of the walls and cut to size with his K-BAR.

There were women's garments cut in military fashion scattered across the floor too, a commando chic that the fashionably punk-minded females of the Nuked Apple thought was the living end instead of a dead end. Phoenix found a pair of fatigue pants and a jacket as he quickly dressed the mannequin to kill.

"Baby," Trench said in a gruff whisper, "you're gonna knock 'em dead."

To make sure of that, Phoenix cut a hunk an inch in diameter off one of the blocks of C-4 plastic explosive from his pack and molded the killy putty to the cycle's rear. A detonator cap went into the center of the putty-like mass, attached to a small electronic timer set to go off in 15 seconds.

Phoenix revved up the Harley and sent it sputtering in the direction of the badass kill crew.

They began firing immediately, aiming at the dummy riding the cycle while Phoenix hightailed it out of the firezone.

The cycle roared out into the street, and the badasses waiting outside behaved as Phoenix had expected they would. While a riderless cycle would have instantly triggered their suspicions and made them break for cover, the sight of a human figure mounted on it would—and did—have the opposite effect.

It would draw their fire and keep them bunched together.

Just like pins at the end of a bowling lane.

The badass leader flashed on what was going down an instant before the C-4 charge detonated with enough impact to blow a 20-foot crater in the street, but not fast enough. As he turned to run, his body was launched through space and torn apart in midair like a carcass on a chopping block, raining back down in bite-size pieces.

Phoenix used the cover of the explosion to sprint through the ground floor of the A&S department store and hustle out the other side, where the badass 4x4 wheelmen were waiting by their parked rigs.

Picking up an empty steel-wire trash can with a sign reading I LOVE NEW YORK on it, Phoenix flung the can into the street. The strategy might have been an oldie, but it was still a goodie. Their nerves frayed from a long wait, the scum boys positioned at the vans opened up on the bouncing, jumping cylindrical object that looked to them like a man sprinting toward them in the split-second it took for them to react.

"Rare, medium, or well-done?" Phoenix asked, jumping out on the van crew's blind side and, without waiting for an answer, opening up with a burst of the

M3P autoshotgun that mowed down the kill crew like so many tin cans.

There were five in all. The guy up front and the two to his right caught the center of the fan of lethal 00 shot, breaking apart like hollow gourds filled with crimson syrup. The other two targets took the edge of the fan across the breadbasket, which had the effect of slicing them in two at the beltline. Their bodies crumpled to the pavement, spraying blood and hunks of abdominal tissue.

Phoenix sprinted for the cab of the first 4x4 and slammed the door behind him. The motor was running and he hammered the gearshift into drive and screamed away from the killzone, heading in the direction he'd started in when the attack had come.

In the rearview, he saw that he still had his dick in the wringer. True, the blast had taken out most of the badass cream machine, but there were enough survivors left to mount a posse howling for his blood.

So far, Phoenix had a solid lead on the street-geek murder crew, but he had no idea how long that lead would be kept up. Phoenix twisted the wheel to keep them off his ass as he burned rubber down Flatbush Avenue, but the badass hit parade was steadily gaining on the 4x4.

The point vehicle, a bizarre hybrid of a Volkswagen and a Barracuda with armor plating and mag wheels, screamed up close, easily doing better than 100 MPH, probably using a nitrogen afterburner.

A dude with a long braid of hair hanging from under the Roman helmet he wore and cigaret-burn eyes leaned out one side of the funny car, hefting a poleax with a blade machined from a hunk of chrome-plated steel that had probably come from a car fender. As the point car came up even with the rear of the fishtailing 4x4, the badass swung the poleax into the side of the truck's cab, its cleaver edge taking a bite out of its metal hide.

While the garbage gladiator slobbered and screamed,

the lead car fell back to the rear of the 4x4 again. Phoenix saw the scum guy execute a daredevil leap from the rear of the funny car onto the roof of his truck.

The highly mobile funny car pulled abreast again. This time the driver leaned across and pointed a wicked-looking sawed-off 12-gauge shotgun at Phoenix.

Glass shattered as the gun went off, shot fragments tearing pieces of skin out of Trench's face. The 4x4 pulled ahead but the faster, more mobile funny car was level with the cab in seconds, the driver leveling the shotgun at Phoenix again.

Phoenix pointed the Ingram 11 and triggered a burst. The driver's head disintegrated. The funny car screeched as death spasms made the crude dude's foot slam hard on the brake and the gas pedal at the same time.

The funny car did a sudden barrel roll, skidding as it turned end-over-end and slamming with incredible momentum into a wall of rubble, where it exploded into a fireball spitting shrapnel everywhere.

Even with the funny car out of commission, Phoenix had his hands full as the blade of the poleax sliced through the roof of the 4x4's cab with the sickening sound of rending metal. The gleaming chrome cutting edge came down almost close enough to give Phoenix a shave. Next time, the maniac on the cab's roof would slice his skull like a grapefruit.

Phoenix leveled the MAC .380 and jerked the trigger in two short, rapid bursts. The gun exploded in his hands, steel whizzers puncturing the roof like tinfoil. There was a demented scream and blood suddenly dripped through the punctures in the roof.

But the badass was still up there. Even with half his belly shot away, he was still high enough and mean enough to crawl forward, holding on against the bucking of the 4x4 and the incredible wind resistance to stick his head into the cab.

"Eat your fucking liver, eat your fucking heart, eat your fucking lungs, eat your fucking—"

A burst blew the head of the demented lunatic into a wet red starburst of bone and brain tissue. Iron-locked fingers went limp on the molding of the truck and the body dropped like a burned-off leech to the rubble, where it rolled and lay still.

Buhh-lammm!

A rocket strike tore up the rubble at the rear of the 4x4, lifting the truck's rear wheels off the ground. Phoenix saw one of the badasses in the three remaining pursuit vehicles fit another mortar round into a rifle barrel, and fire spurt as the bird left the pipe. Another explosion struck, this one even closer to home.

Phoenix felt the truck lurch, heard a loud pop, and then the ear-splitting scraping wail as one of the tires exploded and the truck lurched to its naked rim.

The rim scraped on the ground as the axle sparked against the pavement.

At the same time, Phoenix saw the gas-gauge needle suddenly list to port. That meant only one thing: He'd sprung a leak in his fuel lines.

Throwing open the door, Phoenix jumped from the slowing truck, hitting a pile of rubble with impact that jarred his bones though he rolled with the landing to cushion the force of impact.

Scrambling to bring the M16A2 into firing position, he heard another, louder explosion and the sound of rapid autofire.

Risking a look, Phoenix saw that one of the three badass funny cars was suddenly in flames. Fire spurted from its crippled hulk as two burning figures fell from it, rolling on the ground in their mad frenzy to snuff out the flames which were turning their flesh to brittle charcoal.

Then the car exploded, picking up the thrashing human torches and obliterating them forever.

Badasses were firing from the remaining two chase cars, but not at Phoenix. Their fire was now directed at another vehicle that had roared up behind them. Through the smoke of cordite, Phoenix couldn't make out clearly what it looked like. All he knew right then was that it had saved his ass.

Getting to his feet, Phoenix hefted the M16A2/M203 combo and triggered a FRAG round at one of the remaining chase cars. The badasses exploded in a pillar of smoke and flame. The mystery vehicle mopped up the rest. Most of the street commandos were charred corpses, their cars bits of burning wreckage. The rest cut and ran.

Despite what it had done to the opposition in its unasked-for cavalry charge, Phoenix reloaded and took up a defensive position against the mystery vehicle as it moved slowly through the wreathing smoke and flame of the badass battlezone.

As he watched the battle wagon roll through the smoke, Phoenix was amazed.

What he saw couldn't be happening.

"Imagine running into you here," DeLaCour said, cracking open one of the doors and striding forward, a smoking M60 burp gun propped on one of his massive shoulders, belts of 7.62 ammunition draping his behemoth frame.

Bush Doctor hung his head outside the driver's side window. "You owe me for seven rockets so far," he said, "not counting that first freebie."

"I thought you never go to Brooklyn," Phoenix returned, stepping forward without being able to conceal the surprise and joy he felt at seeing his friends alive.

"There's an exception to every rule," Bush Doctor told him.

17

"See what I mean?" asked Bush Doctor as he passed the probe of the miniaturized metal detector across Phoenix's midsection like some electronic magic wand.

A series of steady shrill pulses were emitted from the base of the probe, getting louder and spaced closer together as Bush Doctor swept the sensor tip across his thigh.

"That little booger is on you somewhere, just a matter of smoking it out."

On a pile at Phoenix's feet were every metal item he had been aware he'd been carrying. He'd even shucked off his high lace-up boots because their steel toes were getting readings from the sensitive probe.

Bush Doctor passed the metal detector's sensor tip across Phoenix's chest, finally zeroing in on his target.

"Gotcha!" he said with glee, as he reached beneath the collar of Trench's flak vest and plucked out an almost invisible sliver of metal which glowed iridescently under the light of the flash Raven held.

"That's how I homed in on you," Bush Doctor went on. "Believe it or not, one of these babies is capable of transmitting across a 20-mile radius."

Phoenix examined the microminiature transmitter which SCORF had slipped on him. He dropped it to the ground and crushed it under his boot heel.

Bush Doctor explained that he had been watching all military traffic in and out of the Liberty Island hard-base, on the off chance that Tallon and Trench had struck a deal.

The cabbie had almost packed it in when he'd seen the Apache helo veer from its usual patrol pattern and vector in on the Diamond District. Bush Doctor's gut instincts immediately told him that Phoenix was on board.

A high-speed drive through the streets of trashed Manhattan confirmed this, and Bush Doctor had followed Phoenix until he'd seen him head down into the subway station.

There was only one place anybody doing that would be bound for. The Wizard's stronghold in Brooklyn, which Abraxas called Oz.

"The little fucker almost didn't tell us," DeLaCour put in. "But we got it out of him."

Bush Doctor smiled sheepishly. "Don't forget that it was me fished your rear ends out of the drink after that chopper exploded," he said.

"Oh, we won't," said Raven. "We won't forget how you charged us for the service either."

From the Ingram SMG riding Bush Doctor's thigh, Phoenix had a good idea of the cabbie's fee. That DeLaCour and Raven had not been killed when the chopper they'd snagged at Liberty Base exploded in midair in a hail of SCORF deathfire was a major miracle.

As it was, the two were half drowned by the time they crawled to shore a half hour later, forced to swim most of the way under the murky surface of the river to avoid the heliborne search crews sent out to find their bodies or take them prisoner.

Chances were, they figured, that Phoenix had gone into Brooklyn, but the only way of getting there in time was to tear ass over the Manhattan Bridge, the only link still existing between Brooklyn and Manhattan.

The only problem was that the bridge was blocked on

the Manhattan side by a contingent of SCORF troopers, and on the Brooklyn side by a small army of heavily armed badasses.

DeLaCour had helped Bush Doctor to transform Li'l Stinky into a heavily armored tank. Steel plate had been welded to its front and rear.

A man-sized hole had been cut in its roof, and around it a three-foot collar of bolted sheet steel had been welded as an M60 machine-gun emplacement.

In their crude but effective war wagon, Bush Doctor, DeLaCour, and Raven had blazed across the Manhattan Bridge into Brooklyn, leaving a trail of badly mangled troopers in their wake.

They had caught up with Phoenix just in time to whale into the tail end of the badass hit crew's sneak attack on Flatbush Avenue.

Now it was night, and they were grouped together against the darkness and the chill like cave people of the future.

None of the three recognized where they were. Nothing was recognizable anymore. It might just as well have been some alien world a million light-years from Planet Earth.

Flatbush Avenue had brought them onto Ocean Parkway, which stretched across the blitzed borough to terminate at Coney Island.

If Coney Island was now the Emerald City of Oz, then Ocean Parkway was the Yellow Brick Road.

It looked more like the road to hell, though.

Along the parkway's sides they had discovered the wreckage of rows of apartment buildings. Though some were still standing more or less intact, most were lying in piles of rubble or had entire sides missing.

Unimaginably powerful nuclear blast waves had produced this effect. While no firestorms had swept through Brooklyn as they had in the other boroughs of the Nuked Apple, the savage toll of the Soviet megatonnage was everywhere.

Strange things were happening here. Hitting the

Parkway, Phoenix and crew took cover as an unearthly motorized procession suddenly screamed down the parkway.

From their vantage points behind the busted foundation wall of an apartment building, the Brooklyn penetration crew witnessed a bizarre motorized joust between two teams of badasses with scavs on the sidelines cheering and whooping as their favorites whacked each other out with crude spears and lances.

They stayed hidden until the tournament broke up with the fall of night, leaving the bodies of the losers to feed the packs of wild dogs, and then scoped out a place to wait until morning, when they hoped to complete the final leg of their journey to meet the Wizard of Oz.

The place they had found was the lower half of one of the apartment buildings which was still fairly whole. Its metal superstructure rose ten stories into the murky sky and then vanished, as though a giant had snapped off the rest and flung it far to the wayside.

The ruined building had an underground garage in its basement, and Bush Doctor had piloted the cab into the gutted lower level of the ruins. In one of the gutted apartments, they found mattresses to sleep on and two cans of Key Food sweet potatoes.

From other apartments they managed to scavenge a brittle copy of *The New York Times*. It was the morning edition that had come out the day the Soviet nukes had dropped. The headline read: BLACK VS. BLACK IN SOUTH AFRICA. There was also a box of kitchen matches, which miraculously still worked, and they took that too to build a fire.

In another apartment, DeLaCour found a carton of strange-looking candles that were inside water glasses with odd labels on them.

"What the hell are these?" DeLaCour asked Phoenix, wondering if they'd be good for providing light.

"They're votive candles," Phoenix returned. "Jews light them to remember their dead."

"In that case we better light the whole box," Raven put in. "There's a lot of dead need remembering."

Back in the underground garage, they had built a fire out of the bits of refuse that had been the furnishings of the homes in which the skeletons which littered this house of death had lived before the nukes exploded.

By the light of the fire, they sat and warmed themselves, passing around the biggest treasure of their expedition—an unopened half-pint bottle of Jack Daniels that had by an incredible stroke of luck been just sitting on the kitchen table of one of the apartments—while Raven turned the feral dog they had killed for the main course on a spit above the crackling flames.

As each tore off strips of the roasted dog's flesh, Phoenix told the others about the reasons for his making the hazardous trek to the blitzed borough through the subway system.

Tallon had given him a choice.

Trade The Child for the lives of his wife and son whom SCORF held prisoners at the Liberty Island hardbase.

"But what's The Child?" asked Bush Doctor, munching on a mouthful of dogmeat. "You talking about grabbing some diaper-wetter?"

"No," said Phoenix. "The Child is a mutant. One of the first genuine mutants to be born after the nuclear war. And one of the few to survive more than a few hours after birth."

The Child was important to SCORF, Phoenix continued, because it was the source of the next best thing to a miracle in the postnuclear hell of America. The Child was the source of a cure for Plague.

"That explains Luther Enoch's interest in getting The Child," Raven said, throwing the last few bones of the dogmeat away into the sputtering flames.

"That it?" asked DeLaCour. "We locate this 'Child' and we get your wife and kid back in exchange?"

"Yeah, I read you," put in Bush Doctor. "But that does not compute. What's to prevent a maggot-shitting hemorrhoid like Tallon from going back on the deal? You say the merc gave you his word of honor. You know what that's worth, don't you?"

Phoenix nodded. He knew very well what Tallon's word was worth. "The merc will deal," Phoenix said. "Not because he can be trusted, but because he and his master know that if they cross me and I live, then they're dead men."

He looked down at the hunk of steaming dogmeat in his hands and bit off another strip of roasted bow-wow. "The real question is, where do I get the right to set up any living thing for a snatch operation, even if it's to get back my wife and son?"

"Well, like my dear old mamma used to say," Bush Doctor opined, scarfing down some more dogmeat, " 'Sometimes you got to smear yourself with shit just to see how many flies you gonna attract.' "

"Yeah." Phoenix responded with a laugh. "I guess that says it all."

have no conception of what a cock was or what it was doing thrusting inside her twat. Somehow, her innocence turned the Wizard on more than the fuck talk and faked orgasms of the most polished street pussy.

The young cooze had done the grunt-and-grind with him for hours, although she had been revolted at the flashburns that had turned his once-handsome face into a road map of hell.

The Latino hooker had no say in the matter, though. Abraxas held the last word in the Emerald City. What he said, went. Whatever shit he wanted to fly, flew.

Buckling the strap of the padded steel mask to the back of his head, Abraxas stood regarding himself in the broken mirror leaning against the wall of an apartment in one of the city housing project towers.

The muscles rippled on the powerful upper torso. The chest was the size of a blockhouse and the arms were like sides of beef. The phallic member was not yet flaccid. Abraxas held it and squeezed its tip until the pain made him wince. Then he dressed quickly and hustled from the room, hearing Melotron giggle behind him as she watched the come wad on her fingertip gleam iridescently in a shaft of sunlight. There was a great deal on the Wizard's mind.

Strangers were coming.

The Lion, the Tin Man, the Scarcrow, and Dorothy.

They were already walking up the Yellow Brick Road. The Child had told him so. The Wizard had looked into The Child's mutant brain and seen them on their way.

Abraxas had to make sure that what they found in the Emerald City was their only way out of Oz.

Total annihilation.

18

Bush Doctor had a hard time accepting that he had to stash his beloved Li'l Stinky before the four of them proceeded any further into Oz. As much as the cabby was attached to his wheels, there was no way the crew would be able to infiltrate the badass hardzone any further in the war wagon.

It would stick out like dogshit on a lace doily.

The Brooklyn warlord's patrols had gotten heavier since their night encampment on Ocean Parkway. The zombie scavs were one thing, but the heavily armed murder crews mounted on their cycles were another matter entirely. Phoenix and company would be stopped and questioned before long, and would have to fight it out.

A firefight wasn't in the cards for a while yet. At least not until they'd soft-probed Abraxas's Coney Island hardbase and found out just who and what The Child was.

On the other hand, if the penetration crew kept their cool, they'd probably be able to blend into the scenery without too much trouble. The trashed streets of the blitzed borough were amazingly full of life. Unlike Manhattan Island, much of Brooklyn still existed as a place where people lived—if you could call what they did living.

Ragged survivors threaded their ways through the chewed-up streets, making for makeshift marketplaces where they could trade for food, clothing, and other necessities. It was a lot, thought Phoenix, like the rough-and-tumble barter towns of the Southwest, where the Dark Messiah's minions had a hands-off policy, allowing local warlords to run their societies in a kind of neo-feudalism.

Only here in Nuked York City the contrast was overwhelming. Just a few miles across the river, where SCORF ruled the blasted streets of what had once been the city's glittering but diamond-hard heart, nothing but chaos prevailed. Yet in Brooklyn, where the chance misfiring of a Soviet nuke meant to obliterate the borough had instead saved much of it, and given the warlord a power base which SCORF had decided not to challenge, a semblance of workaday life still continued.

Before the sun rose—its face stained a hellfire red by the swirling dust particles of nuclear detonations cycling through the upper atmosphere—the Phoenix team had scouted out a place to stash Bush Doctor's wheels where Li'l Stinky had a small chance of staying safe while the strike crew proceeded on its mission deep in the heart of chaos.

The stash site was a Sanitation Department depot that was full of the rotting hulks of garbage trucks and street sweepers. The derelict trash wagons provided just the right camouflage for Bush Doctor's cab. It was also an easy landmark to spot, in case the strike crew needed some motorized transport out of Brooklyn in a hurry.

"Okay, Li'l Stinky," Bush Doctor said to his wheels before leaving the cab. "Daddy's gonna be gone for awhile now. You just sit tight and keep cool. He'll be back for you before long." Tears were in his eyes. The cabbie actually related to his cab like a living thing.

Bush Doctor nodded to the rest of the team after saying his fond farewell, and they saddled up and began moving through the jagged streets of a nuclear dawn.

All around them was the awesome devastation

wreaked by the explosions of N-Day. Although the nuke meant to destroy Brooklyn had exploded out in the Atlantic, it had exploded close enough to shore to generate fierce blast waves which collapsed flimsier houses like stacks of playing cards and severely damaged even heavier multi-story brick buildings.

Manhattan had been worse off by far. The Soviet warhead had detonated with perfect accuracy six miles above the center of the long, narrow island, its ferocious shock waves reducing the heart of New York City to a radioactive wasteland.

Cut off from the heart of the city, Brooklyn had to revert to a state of primitive barter and farming a lot like that which prevailed in the western states, where nuke damage had been minimal compared with the total collapse of American society—a collapse which had proven just as devastating as a direct nuclear strike in many ways.

Here, like there, the borough found itself ruled by the strongest of the warlords who survived the nuke attack, a hardnosed shogun whose leadership cut both ways, providing the survivors which a modicum of central government, yet demanding total obedience. Those who didn't want to live under those conditions either had to go elsewhere or shut up.

In the flattened cityscape around them the intact projects of Coney Island looked like some distant landmark. In the light of early morning, torches lit the brick monoliths, which rose eerily against the red horizon. The smoky wind carried on it the screams and shouts of denizens of the nukeworld as they lived and died in the wasteland around them.

Phoenix and company had no difficulty in making out their destination. Phoenix estimated that it would take them the better part of the day to reach Abraxas's Coney Island strongbase on foot.

There was a better way, though.

The elevated subway line seemed to be intact as well. The elevated tracks stretched across the borough, creating a direct link between the penetration crew and Coney Island. Phoenix shaded his eyes and looked across the wasted lunar expanse as a train chugged across the elevated tracks, the diesel locomotive pulling it leaving behind a plume of smoke. He could hear its whistle blowing eerily in the dim light.

Scavs watched the heavily armed warriors move through the wasteland toward the elevated subway line as the early morning sun cast a faint warmth over the trashed landscape. They had walked no more than an hour before reaching one of the elevated's stations, and trudged up the stairs toward the mezzanine.

Badasses armed with rifles waited inside, guarding the entrance to the rows of turnstiles. Other passengers were ahead of them, standing in a small line.

Phoenix watched as a woman dressed in filthy, foul-smelling rags reached into a dirty handbag and took out a videotape cassette. She handed it to one of the armed badasses who guarded the turnstiles and looked on apprehensively as he inspected the tape.

"Tracy Lords, huh," the mouth-breather said. A smile creased his ugly mug as he handed the tape to the other gorilla standing next to him. "You got anything else?" he asked.

The woman shook her head and clutched the young child standing beside her close to her body.

"Okay," said the badass. "You go through." The woman hustled through the turnstiles, scuttling through the doors and up the stairs to the platform beyond as if she wanted to get it done before the hardguy had a chance to change his mind.

An old man stood in front of the Phoenix team. The guy wore a bunch of rags that had once been a 700-dollar Burberry raincoat. Plastic bags had been tied around his ripped shoes for insulation. His beard was gray and his eyes looked like they were floating in cherry syrup.

"I'm a poet," the guy told the turnstile toll collectors. "All I got to give you is a poem."

This remark brought a smile to the face of one of the badasses. He turned to the crude dude bracketing him at the other side of the turnstile row.

"You hear that, Sharky?" he asked his partner. "Salami Lips here says he wants to recite us a fuckin' poem."

"Maybe the guy can tap-dance?" the other badass replied. "No poem any fuckin' good without some tap dancin' to go with it. See if the old fucker can do us a soft shoe, then maybe we can let him through."

"Hear that, Pops?" asked the first guard. "You do us a tap dance and we'll listen to your poem. We'll even give you some music, won't we, Sharky?"

"Oh, yeah, sure," Sharky said, whipping out a Colt .357 Python and cocking its trigger. "I got the perfect tap dancin' music for ya, Pops."

Badass Two pointed the Python at the old man and squeezed off a round. The hardnose bullet sparked as it zinged off the concrete deck a fraction of an inch from the old man's plastic-bagged shoes. He jumped back and threw up his hands.

The two badasses guffawed.

"Play it again, Sharky," Badass One hollered. "A little up-tempo this time."

His pard obliged, loosing another round that made the old man hop backwards.

"Okay, that's enough," the first badass said. "Don't wanna run out of ammunition, do we, Sharky?" Turning to the old man, he asked, "Now give us a little bit of poetry. We gotta improve our minds, don't we?"

The old man composed himself. "This poem is called 'Mondo Bullwhip.' " He pulled a torn book from his pocket and began reading:

> Hiding what lies behind the armor's chinks, writhing on its cross. Hanging from subway straps, they emerge from their pupal skins. Metamorphosis complete they dry their iridescent wings and buzz into the twilight. They have developed

> beyond the needs of mere flesh. They are mineral intelligences. Pure. Glacial. Bent on annihilation.

Badass One made a farting sound. His scuzzbag pard broke up with laughter.

"Okay, okay," he said. "Enough with the poetry. Getcha ass outta here, and next time you bring something *real* to trade for your ride or we make you eat that motheaten book of bullshit, okay, Pops?"

The old poet shuffled feebly through the doors and up the stairs leading to the platform.

"Whadda you got, pal?" asked the guard of Phoenix. His eyes darted to Raven, who was standing directly behind Phoenix, and he smacked his lips. "Maybe the squeeze got something she can trade, huh?"

"Yeah—like her pussy!" his brother rat chimed in.

Phoenix snap-kicked the guard in the midsection, breaking his jaw with a backfist punch on the follow-through. His pard had whipped a pump-action shotgun at Phoenix, but DeLaCour and Raven already had the dude pinned in their weapons' line of fire.

Hauling the injured badass to his feet, Phoenix slam-danced him up against the iron gate that divided the mezzanine into two unequal sections.

"What the fuck did you want?" he asked the badass, who was puking blood.

"Nuh-nuthin' . . ." groaned the injured guard. "Di-didn't want nuthin' at all."

"But *I* want something," Phoenix growled. "I want you to give *me* something, you puke-breathing wad of gorilla come. I want something from you." For emphasis, Phoenix slammed the punk over the turnstile, forcing the hard metal edge of the turnstile into the small of the hardguy's back.

"What?" asked the scared-shitless havoc ranger. "You're crazy. Whaddaya want from me?"

"You tell me."

"Hey, look, I—" Phoenix slammed him even harder,

hearing his spine crunch.

"Tell me what I want," he pressed.

The guard's eyes bugged in his blood-drained face.

"You want me to let you ride for free. You and your pards, right? Okay, you ride for free."

"That's part of it, pal," Phoenix said, relaxing his hold a little. "What's the rest?"

The guard thought for a moment. "You want me to apologize to the lady. Yeah, okay. I apologize. Sure, anything you want. Sure. I apologize, yeah, sure."

Phoenix hauled the badass up by the collar of his leather jacket and flung him halfway across the mezzanine. Cracking open the guy's weapon, he removed the bullets and threw them on the floor. Phoenix, DeLaCour, Raven, and Bush Doctor vaulted the turnstiles and walked up the stairs. Slow. The rest of the people behind them rode free that morning.

The subway train rumbled as it rolled into the station, sounding two hoots on its horn. The six cars were rusted and stained by the elements. They were pulled by the locomotive of a Transit Authority work train. The small diesel had been pressed into service along the rails which were no longer electrified. It was slow and dirty, but it worked.

Along with the Phoenix team, a gaggle of scavs waited on the platform for the train to pull in. The train made the elevated run between Church Avenue and the Stillwell Avenue Station at Coney Island, its last stop. After they took seats and the train pulled out, a vendor came into the car, hawking snacks and drinks.

"Get your dogmeat-on-a-stick," he cried, "get your fresh roasted dogmeat-on-a-stick!"

Bush Doctor ordered a dogmeat popsicle and a bottle of Brain Tumor, a locally bottled beer. As Bush Doctor offered Raven a bite, Phoenix noticed the old poet sitting at the other end of the car, reading from his book of verse.

"You smoke?" Phoenix asked, producing a pack of

Marlboro filter tips given to him by Tallon, and watching the old man's eyes light up at the sight of the rare tobacco. "Go ahead, take one," he said at the old poet's hesitance to touch the cigaret.

The old man lit up and dragged deep, sucking the smoke into his lungs. "What you want from me?" he asked Phoenix. "I only got my poems."

"What's your name, old man?" Phoenix asked.

"You can call me Ishmael," the poet returned.

Phoenix smiled. "I want a poem, old man. Tell me a poem about The Child."

Ishmael's face took on a crafty look. "You ain't from around here?" he asked. "You from someplace different."

"The Child," Phoenix pressed. "What do you know about it?"

"The Child is the day and he is the night," Ishmael answered. "The Child heals and he takes away. He is everything and he is nothing. That's all I know."

"One more thing," Phoenix asked before turning away. "Where is The Child?"

"The old city projects," returned Ishmael. "That's where the hellspawned abomination lives."

19

At the end of the line stood Coney Island. Not the Coney Island of a lifetime ago, thought Magnus Trench. Not the place he had cut classes at Franklin Delano Roosevelt High School to go to ride the roller-coaster and the ferris wheel and eat hot dogs at Nathan's—but a new and different place, a place which its warlord, Abraxas, called Oz.

Here at land's end, where high winds flecked the steely ocean with whitecaps as the red gong of the sun slipped silently into its watery grave, there was a rowdy freehold where anything and everything was bought and sold.

Surf Avenue divided the giant concrete towers of the project from the Astroland amusement park, which still looked amazingly like its prewar self, though there were changes which left Trench with no illusions. He hadn't come through a time warp. That was then and this was now, no doubt about it.

Along Surf Avenue, the makeshift stalls of street hustlers selling goods of every description had replaced the amusement arcades and heartburn-Valhalla eateries. The streetlamps were gone, and torches flickered in the cold ocean breeze, illuminating the night world with a flickering glow.

Crowds of scavs, dressed in the bizarre fashions of

postnuclear America, thronged the crowded thoroughfare. Heavy leather gleamed on their bodies and spiked chains clinked threateningly as they walked, their body language challenging any onlookers.

All were armed, and those who couldn't afford firearms carried long, wickedly sharp machetes in scabbards at their waists.

Whores of both sexes worked the crowds, openly soliciting sex and performing it in any convenient place, often as crowds of spectators watched and joined in at their pleasure. The mutant hookers seemed to be especially popular, especially those with both male and female genitalia. Phoenix noticed a pair of Siamese twins going down on a badass and his pet dog simultaneously.

In addition to the booths of the sellers of wares, there were booths in which curiosities of every sort could be seen. Here was something called an "I'V. Parlor." Zombie scavs, with eyes that were burned out cinders and intravenous packs taped to their bodies dripping continuous dosages of LSD into their veins, shambled into the building that had once been a branch of Manufacturers Hanover Trust.

The I.V. Parlor was next door to Shock Therapy City. Through its plateglass window Phoenix could see the denizens of Oz lined up to lie on a metal table and have their frontal lobes juiced with thousands of volts of electricity. They would thrash and buck, then stumble away, their pain and misery temporarily forgotten as their frontal lobes were numbed.

Rememberers had set up booths at various points throughout the thoroughfare, and they were obviously doing bang-up business, to judge by the number of scavs who queued up to hear stories about how Nuked York City once was.

Badmouthers had their booths set up too. For a fee, which could either be in coin of the realm or bartered goods, the badmouthers would scream and curse and beat their chests about the obliteration of the world.

Most scavs found listening to badmouthers soothing.

A Human Worm fight was being held behind a roped-off area, and scores of scavs cheered on their favorites. The armless, legless Human Worms thrashed around in the dirt, each trying to bite into the other's jugular and win a night of lust with a mutant hooker.

A group of Hare Krishnas stood by chanting, across the street from a bunch of Whirling Dervishes in front of the Moonie Church, a former Kentucky Fried Chicken joint.

Badasses packing heavy heat rumbled through the crowds in Brinks armored trucks which had been taken from a local garage, their eyes warily scanning the throngs of passersby for any hint of trouble. One patrol locked on the Phoenix crew, but it slid away seemingly without any sign of recognition.

Torches lit the amusement park fairway, and the Loew's movie theater's marquee advertised a double feature consisting of *Back To Bataan,* starring John Garfield, and *Deep Throat,* starring Linda Lovelace.

Phoenix, DeLaCour, Raven, and Bush Doctor checked out some of the signs on the stalls lining Surf Avenue, wondering what the hell they could mean.

SPACE FUCK

PISS ON THE FAT LADY

THE ULTIMATE IN SMOKING PLEASURE

SNAKEFIST MUFFINS

BOFF A DEAD PIG FETUS

LOBOT-O-RAMA

WORLD WAR FOOD

"I don't know about the rest of those joints,"

DeLaCour put in, "but if that last place sells eats, I'm for checking it out."

World War Food turned out to be the legendary Nathan's franks and ribs emporium. Only under new ownership. Before N-Day some said that it had served the best franks, burgers, fries, and ribs in town. Now the fare was a little different and somewhat more colorfully named.

Dogmeat, ground fresh from bow-wows raised in kennels nearby, had replaced beef in the franks, and although ice-cold Budweiser was no longer available due to a lack of both refrigeration and Bud, hot Spinal Tap, a local brew, was available in draft or bottles. Scavs lined up at World War Food's counter to scarf down their dogs and Spinal Tap suds by the dozens.

"What'll it be?" asked the counterman, a dude wearing a black rubber SCUBA suit with a nylon stocking pulled over his face and a red bandana tied around the top of the stocking mask.

"Whaddaya got?"

The masked counterman ran down the menu for DeLaCour.

"We got Blitz Burgers, Cowpox Pizza, Last Gasp Tacos, Homicide Falafal, and our world-famous Triple Decker Rigor Mortis Hero Sandwich."

"Whaddaya got to drink besides Spinal Tap?"

"Hot Gorilla Piss with a twist of bullshit, diet or regular."

While DeLaCour munched his Rigor Mortis Hero, he watched the badmouther's booth across the street where the guy was going into his act. After getting paid with a necklace made from precious pre-war beer-bottle glass strung on unwaxed dental floss, the badmouther began thrashing around on the floor, cutting his face and hands with a double-edged razor blade.

"They killed us all!" he screamed as a crowd looked on. "They blew us up. God damn them. *Damn the crazy fuckers.* What have they done to us? Where is justice? *Where?"*

Tears came to the eyes of the assembled scavs. Most of them burst into applause. The badmouther got up and took a bow, wiped the blood off his body, and serviced another customer.

"How about a Necrofurter?" Phoenix asked Raven and Bush Doctor. "Maybe they even have sauerkraut?"

The guy slapped the dogs on the counter and slid two rewashed paper cups full of Gorilla Piss at them, regular for Phoenix, diet for Raven. The food wasn't half bad. Didn't have sauerkraut, though.

"What the hell's that?" asked Bush Doctor, pointing at what looked like a procession of people gripping torches who were moving off Surf Avenue toward the projects.

Phoenix asked the counterman.

"Some kind of religious bullshit. Cripples. Freaks," he said cryptically, and turned back to his dogfurters.

Having scarfed down his food, and having asked around on his own, Bush Doctor returned to the rest of the crew and said, "They gonna see The Child."

The penetration team exchanged looks. Anywhere The Child was, they were going to go.

Pulling DeLaCour away from a whore who was kneeling at his feet with his cock in her mouth, the crew took off in the direction of the torchlit procession.

It was made up of scores of people. Their eyes were gleaming orbs which stared mesmerized as they shuffled toward the projects which rose against the surreal horizon.

Most of these scavs were diseased. Plague blisters and Herpes-3 pustules covered their faces, and their bodies had been disfigured into hideous caricatures of the human beings they once had been.

They were the religious pilgrims of the postnuclear Endtimes, questing after a miracle cure for the afflictions that had befallen them without their having been responsible.

Here a mother clutched a child that resembled a

lizard, its flesh scaled and a tail whipping from beneath the rags which swaddled it. Here Siamese twins, their bodies crippled and warped, shuffled toward the concrete towers.

They came crawling in their own slime, their bodies mere atrophied remains of the human body. They came hopping on one foot, and they came flip-flopping on none.

They came with tendrils in place of arms and legs, and with hair that had been replaced with feathers, and with sexual organs enlarged to bizarre giantism. They came without mouths and without eyes and even without brains in their hydrocephalic skulls.

Locked together like hideous snakes they came. Crawling on their bellies, their bodies segmented like worms, they came. They came with bat wings and with elephant ears and with the skin missing from their faces so the muscle tissue and the network of veins was visible on the surface.

All of them came looking for that age-old fix.

Salvation.

Torches flickered in the blown-out windows of the projects, and armed figures were etched against the sky on the rooftops.

Surrounding the procession were squads of armed leather uglies, their weapons sweeping back and forth across the crowd.

"Walk quietly to see The Child," one of them said through a bullhorn, addressing the masses. "Keep in line, single file. The Child will answer your questions."

Salvation had its price. Before they entered The Child's domain, the house of their mini-God, they gave their donations into one of the large metal barrels outside. At a nod from one of the gun-toting uglies, they filed inside. There The Child would heal them. Or so they believed.

Suddenly there was the sound of jingling.

Phoenix turned and saw a dwarf capering toward him. The dwarf wore a jester's outfit. Shoes with curled toes, shirt with balloon sleeves, pointy cap, the whole routine. The jingling came from the bells on the dwarf's feet and cap.

"Faraway's the name," the dwarf said as he ran up to Phoenix and tugged at the fabric of his fatigue pants. "I bring you tidings from my master Abraxas, the Wizard of Oz."

"Get lost, maggot," Bush Doctor said to the dwarf, raising his foot as if to kick him aside.

"Judge me not by my size," said Faraway, unruffled by Bush Doctor's display. "Nor by the clothes on my back, for Faraway is a man both of means and of intelligence. Judge me only by the caliber of my weapon."

"What the hell kind of rap is that?" asked DeLaCour.

"I think he's cute," Raven said.

"Thank you, milady," Faraway told her. "And Faraway thinks you've got a righteous sweet ass."

"Okay, short stuff," Phoenix said. "Cut the bullshit. What's your spiel?"

"Faraway knows why you have come to the Emerald City of Oz. You have come to see The Child," he replied. "Faraway will take you to The Child. He will arrange a private audience."

"Why should we trust you, roach prick?" DeLaCour asked. "I mean a guy in that bozo outfit you got on don't exactly spark undying trust."

The dwarf smiled.

A MAC 11 SMG was suddenly in the diminutive jester's hands.

"Faraway doesn't need trust when he has a piece, asshole," he snorted, the smile growing broader. "Like I told you twerps before, 'Judge me only by the caliber of my weapon.' "

Instantly, there came the telltale clicks of breech bolts snapping hard on the firing chambers of automatic weapons. Phoenix and crew looked around at a brace of hardguys converging on them from every direction.

"Move!" shouted Phoenix to Raven as he cut loose a barrage of SMG quickbursts in rapid succession to cover their dash for freedom. Raven and Bush Doctor hightailed it out of the firezone. They disappeared into the crowds milling around in the plaza of the projects.

Phoenix and DeLaCour were surrounded by a crew of hardguys with their weapons trained on them.

"Abraxas welcomes you," Faraway said, holstering the MAC. "He welcomes you to the Emerald City of Oz."

20

The Wizard of Oz sat on his throne at the center of the tent. If the throne looked a lot like a dentist's chair, that's because it was.

Abraxas had glommed the chair from the Coney Island Dental Clinic. It was a modern chair made of hand-dyed kidskin that could be raised and lowered by remote control. Abraxas liked the way it felt.

The tent had all kinds of stuff inside it. Its interior decoration was a crazy-quilt hodgepodge of goods stolen from the interiors of furniture showrooms across the borough. Italian Modern stood cheek-by-jowl with French Provincial. But it was all good stuff. Used to be the best that money could buy. Now the best that heisters could steal.

Blazing in sconces set into the walls, torches cast eerie flickers over the tent's interior. Even though the Wizard of Oz had his own generator, he liked the effect of torchlight. Gave the joint a touch of the macabre.

Faraway capered ahead of the prisoners as Phoenix and the steel-faced giant named DeLaCour were led in at gunpoint, their hands shackled behind their backs.

"Your humble servant has brought you the intruders, Wiz," said Faraway, leaping nimbly to the dais on which Abraxas's throne stood and jingling a tambourine as he went into his rap. "You see before you the Cowardly Lion and the Tin Man. The Scarecrow and Dorothy have escaped, for the nonce, but will soon be apprehended."

"Don't give me a brain tumor, you little rat prick," Abraxas said to Faraway. "Like everybody else in the Emerald City, you do what you're told. And quit talking like Shakespeare. It gives me heartburn."

Jumping onto Abraxas's lap, the jester rapped his tiny knuckles across on the steel mask which obscured the badass warlord's hideously flashburned face from the world.

"Knock, knock. Who's there?" asked Faraway. "Why it's the face of Old Mister Death himself," he answered.

"Don't push your fucking luck, little man," Abraxas said in a gruff voice to the dwarf. "One day I'll have your balls for bookends."

But Faraway wasn't listening. Jumping off the Wizard's lap, he began capering around the heels of the two captives.

"Let me set them on fire, master! Gasoline and honey. So it sticks to their bodies and the fire burns right through their flesh and cooks their organs inside their bodies," Faraway cried out, whipping the tiny submachine gun from under his gaudy jester's suit.

"Please let me rip out their eyeballs with my teeth and set their bodies on fire. Then I could jerk off into the flames!"

"Shut your face, cockroach," Abraxas hollered at the fool. "The rest of you take a hike," he said to the crew of badasses jamming their weapons into Phoenix and DeLaCour's backs.

Moments later Abraxas was alone with his captives.

"I know why you have come," the warlord said to the prisoners. "You have come to take The Child." Abraxas got up from his throne and strode across the space to Phoenix and DeLaCour.

A big man, Abraxas stood nose-to-nose with his prisoners. He looked Phoenix straight in the eye.

"I know who you are too," Abraxas said. "The Child has shown me brain videos."

"Who am I?" asked Phoenix, knowing that the guy was a psycho. Like all the others who had survived the nuke graveyard and emerged to positions of power, Abraxas didn't have every wheel touching the ground anymore—if he ever did.

"You are the man they say can't be killed. You are a legend. You stand against the Dark Messiah and his merc commandos who feast off the corpse of this once-great city like maggots on a dead man's grave. In short, you are the Cowardly Lion. That is why you have been allowed to follow the Yellow Brick Road. That is why you are here, now, speaking to me in the heart of my domain."

The problem was, what would Abraxas do now? The warlord wasn't sure. He figured he might be able to hold the Lion and the Tin Man for ransom, but would anybody want to pay it?

Suddenly Faraway jumped up and whispered in Abraxas's ear. Phoenix and DeLaCour saw him nod and stroke his chin as he considered the jester's words. Abraxas finally nodded to Faraway.

"May I tell them, Wiz?" Faraway asked, jumping up and down so that the bells on his costume jingled crazily. "May I tell them of their ultimate fate? Oh, please, Wiz of Wizzes, let Faraway pass judgment on the intruders!"

Abraxas flicked his finger at the dwarf. Faraway nodded his head and clapped his tiny hands in demented glee at this sign to proceed.

"My master, the great and powerful Abraxas, Wizard of Oz, commands me to inform the Cowardly Lion and the Tin Man without a heart that you will both be given the chance to die like heroes in the ultimate contest. If you survive, you will be taken to The Child, and The Child will decide whether you live or die."

"There, over that way, Cutter!" one of the gruff

voices hollered. "I swear I saw the fuckers duck down behind that building wall!"

There was more swearing, and then the sound of boot leather slapping rubble as the hit-paraders ran off into the darkness, leaving their quarry hunkering only a few feet below.

Raven and Bush Doctor had hauled ass through the lunatic night, past the decaying concrete of the busted highway, searching for a place to hole up and plan their next move.

The name of the game so far had been shake your shit and don't get hit. But they were tired of dodging bullets and too out-of-breath to do anything but find a nice dark hole to crawl into.

The badass kill crew that had chased them from the housing project ambush had stayed on them like stink on shit for the better part of an hour, throwing fire at everything that moved.

Fortunately, they'd been as short on brains as they'd been quick on the trigger. Raven and Bush Doctor had managed to ditch the hollering, whooping chase crew by throwing a few pieces of junk off the ground at a pack of wild dogs, making them scatter into the shadows of the deepening twilight.

The hunched shapes moving dimly against the horizon had been enough to confuse the Wizard's gun-toting goon crew.

But although they'd shaken the badass kill crew that had chased them from the housing projects, they both were painfully aware that the shit had just begun to fly.

"What we gonna do now?" Bush Doctor asked.

"Break them out," Raven answered, her jaw set and a hard light in her icy blue eyes. "Or kill ourselves trying."

Blastroland, read the sign.

Thousands of denizens of Oz jammed the amusement park's bleachers. Torches lit up the night as the prisoners were brought out in a bizarre procession.

Beyond it was the roller-coaster ride and the ferris wheel and the fairway with its booths filled with geeks.

The big neon sign at one side of the roller coaster had once read CYCLONE. But the first two letters had been burned out. Now its blinking letters spelled out:

C—L—O—N—E

Faraway led the guards, who force-marched the shackled Phoenix to a car of the roller coaster. The crowd pressed in on either side, spitting at him and jeering loudly. Behind Phoenix, a crew of four badass bikers piled into the other car.

Unlike Phoenix they were heavily armed.

"Ladies and gentlemen of Oz," Faraway began, speaking into a microphone, his amplified voice ringing out over the amusement park. "Welcome to Blastroland, the place where all your fantasies come true. Tonight," he continued, "we proudly bring you another battle to the death on Clone."

The crowd cheered wildly, applauding and whistling. Faraway gestured toward the right. A spotlight fell across the roller coaster.

"In this corner, we have Phoenix the Cowardly Lion, who will test his mettle against a crowd of violencers on the death course called Clone."

More applause.

Faraway gestured at the Wonder Wheel to his right. A spotlight picked out DeLaCour, who was chained between two of the hoppers.

"The Tin Man is in the other corner," Faraway said with glee. "Which contestant will live? Which contestant will die? Before the night is over you will all know the answer. As the Tin Man's will to live is tested on the Thunder Wheel.

"Please, please!" the dwarf jester cried, waving his arms to hold down the noise of applause and cheers. "There's more to be heard, good people of Oz!" When the noise level died down, Faraway continued: "Witness

Clone. Truly, it is a gauntlet rivaling the most fabled of fact or fiction, present or past.

"See the Pit of Fire!" Faraway went on, gesturing as flames suddenly leapt to life through the loop-the-loop at the top of the roller coaster, created by a flame-thrower-packing badass. "Through this blazing inferno Phoenix will have to pass as he is whirled at death defying speeds across Clone!"

More applause.

"See the Peak of Destiny!" Faraway gestured at the crest of the roller coaster, where a brace of badasses manned a .50-caliber Browning machine-gun nest.

"Through this storm of lethal lead the Cowardly Lion will travel after passing through the Pit of Fire." The spotlight fell on the machine-gunners, who cut loose a full-auto volley to the delight of the capacity audience.

"And all the while, Phoenix will be chained to his car, hotly pursued by these fierce warriors you now see before you!"

A four-man badass crew stepped forward into the spotlight's glare. The hardguy hit crew packed lethal full-auto weapons and spat at Phoenix as they passed his car.

"Last but not least," the dwarf jester went on, "our brave hero Phoenix will be armed with only the crudest weapons.

He picked up a shield made of the hood of a Cadillac —the hood ornament was still there—and chucked it into Phoenix's car. The shield was followed by a sword made out of the axle of a Chevy.

"Let's have a real big hand for Phoenix, the Cowardly Lion!" Faraway said. "Win or lose, he's a hell of a guy!"

Faraway let the applause die down. Now the spotlight fell on DeLaCour, who was chained to the center of the Thunder Wheel.

"But let's not leave out our other brave warrior," the dwarf continued. "The Tin Man. A freak of nature. His body half flesh, half stainless-steel plate, his face a hideous mask riveted to the bones of his face. Yet let not this monstrosity's appearance fool you. They say the Tin Man has no heart, yet inside he has the courage of a tiger—as you will all soon discover when the Tin Man's mettle is tested to the ultimate on The Thunder Wheel!"

More applause.

"Observe the Thunder Wheel. Chained to its center is The Tin Man. As he revolves with the slowly turning wheel, warriors of Oz will test his courage with stabs and jabs of their long spears, sharp sickles, and razor-edged swords.

"How long will the Steel Man survive?" Faraway asked. "The answer depends on Phoenix, for if the Cowardly Lion can escape, he will be able to free the Tin Man, rescuing his brave friend and staunch comrade from a grisly death.

"But now." Faraway paused and let the silence ring for awhile. "*Let the games begin!*"

Part 4:
Ride the Lightning

21

The crowd exploded into a turbulent spasm of applause.

The car sprang forward, gravity hurling Phoenix back into his seat as it swept up the first of Clone's hairpin curves.

Craning his neck, Phoenix looked behind him but didn't see the second car—the chase car full of heavily armed badasses—launched after him yet.

As the car gained momentum, climbing up a steep French curve, he understood why.

Bratatatatatatatatatat!

The obscene hiccuping of full-auto weapons shattered the night, and the torching flashes of their muzzles revealed the hunched manshapes positioned across the tortuously twisting roller-coaster course.

This would only be the first round. The slimesuckers would parade him around the course first, shooting high, not intending to kill or even wound.

The killing and wounding would come soon enough, though.

Phoenix raised the shield and ducked as a cluster of lead tumblers ricocheted off the thick iron slab, the impact feeling like men were smashing clubs against the shield.

The car was picking up speed, climbing up toward the crest of the roller coaster, and from the stands below Phoenix heard the crowd break into more applause as another hardcase punk equipped with an automatic shotgun sprayed a hot-metal geyser across Phoenix's car.

As he passed out of the fan of lethal shot and reached the highest point of Clone, Phoenix was able to squint beneath the shield and see DeLaCour's body chained to the Thunder Wheel, turning around as he tried to fight off the bloodthirsty badass rat pack trying to hack him to pieces.

Suddenly the car began its descent down a steep incline, picking up speed and crushing Phoenix hard against the seat. Up ahead was a loop-the-loop. The car screamed down the slope, gaining momentum and then shot up into the loop-the-loop like a stone from a slingshot.

Upside down now, Phoenix saw another badass level a flamethrower and squirt a long plume of incinerating napalm at him. He barely got his shield up in time to deflect the fire stream before shooting out of the loop-the-loop and back down another steep incline.

More hardcase punks were posted on the rest of the trip, shooting over Phoenix's head, instructed not to kill the contestant yet. The crowd below again went wild as Phoenix came hurtling down toward them at breakneck speed, giving him a standing ovation.

"Let's hear it for Phoenix!" Faraway's voice screamed over the public-address system. "Whatta great guy! Whatta great guy!"

This time it was going to be for real, Phoenix knew, as momentum carried the car past the embarkation area and once again up the first of Clone's many steep and tortuous curves, to begin the run all over again.

As he crested the first of these and began a steep descent more than 20 feet in depth, he heard the crowd roar from below and knew the second car full of badasses had been launched in hot pursuit.

Raven and Bush Doctor approached Blastroland cautiously from its blind side, away from Surf Avenue and toward the beach. Only a single sentry had been posted there, and he presented no problem in being taken out.

"Who's that?" the sentry challenged, bobbing his neck in an attempt to see into the shrouding darkness. "Lemme get a look at you or I'll shoot first and ask my questions later."

Raven stepped out of the shadows. The guard's jowly, unshaven face broke into a leering grin as he took in her jutting breasts and long black hair.

"Don't fire," Raven said, coming closer. "I was only—"

The guard's leer grew even larger, and he let his weapon drop. "Yeah, I know what you were doing on the beach," he said. "Suckin' some dude's prick."

Motioning her forward, the guard went on, "You suck my cock and I'll give you a chocolate bar. Hershey's. Got it right here." The guard patted the breast pocket of the shirt he wore—a ruffle-front dress shirt that was covered with grime and fastened at the wrists with safety pins instead of cufflinks.

"Real chocolate?" Raven asked, feigning surprise.

"Yup," said the guard. "Real as it gets."

The guard's arms were suddenly pinned behind him as Bush Doctor jumped out of the shadows.

Raven whipped a nine-inch stainless-steel pigsticker from the waistband of her camos and plunged it into the guard's abdomen. The sentry's eyes bugged as he went into convulsions, and Raven had to keep her hand over his mouth as he tried to scream, the blood pumping from his throat pouring hot and thick through the spaces of her fingers.

When the kicking and thrashing finally stopped, they let the sentry fall to the sandy ground.

"Shit!" Bush Doctor said, rifling the pockets of the corpse's fatigues. "That scumbag lied. There ain't no Hershey bar in here!" He kicked the corpse in the side, the steel toe of his boot shattering the deadman's ribs.

"Come on," Raven told him, grabbing Bush Doctor by the arm. "We got work to do."

Covered by the noise of the crowd, Raven and the cabbie unsheathed the C-4 and TNT charges they had prepared to blow half of the amusement park to kingdom come. It was admittedly a strategy of last resorts, but at this point any strategy was preferable to none at all.

The diversion would at least give Phoenix and DeLaCour enough precious moments to make a run for it. If they were successful in getting away from their traps, they might just be able to hook up with Raven and Bush Doctor and escape from Coney Island with their skins intact.

But Raven knew that wouldn't be good enough for Phoenix. Magnus Trench was a man obsessed. He would still want to see The Child.

Autofire sprang off the rear of the speeding roller coaster car as Phoenix was whipped around a death curve on the cyclone ride to hell.

He ducked sideways, going against the momentum of the car as it jogged fiercely left, evading a lancet of lead that would have torn his head off at the neck had he not done so.

He was now no more than halfway through his second run around the course and gaining momentum for the steep climb to the peak of Clone, before entering the slalom run that would shoot him 20 feet down before shooting him up again to the deadly loop-the-loop.

This time Phoenix knew that the scum beings manning the flamethrower would be shooting to kill. At the same time the goon crew chasing him in the car behind him would be aiming to blow him into eternity.

Talk about no-win situations.

The car shot up the steep incline under a hailstorm of razoring steel and belching flame, crested the top of the tracks, teetered for the briefest instant, and then plunged quickly down.

Phoenix kept his head down and his shoulders tucked forward, minimizing the surface area that stuck out above the car and decreasing his chances of catching a bullet in a vital area.

Plunging down the slope, the car reached bottom and shot up again into the loop-the-loop as, scenting blood, the crowd cheered wildly at the bottom of the run.

An arc of flame whooshed from the thrower's nozzle as the torchman at the Pit of Fire opened up full throttle. Phoenix hunched down beneath the shield, feeling the broiling river of fire wash over him, keeping his feet hooked under the seat as he felt himself turned upside down with a sickening wrench as the car spun around the inside of the loop-the-loop and turned bottom up.

The heat was incredible. It turned the iron shield red hot. Phoenix felt the skin of his arm and hand blister and breathed the odor of his own roasting hair and flesh. In addition to this punishment, he had to strain every muscle in his body to keep from tumbling from the car.

Despite the excruciating pain, Phoenix knew that if he lightened up on the shield for only the briefest second, the flaming liquid would stick to his body like burning glue.

It would eat into his flesh in seconds, penetrating his

heart and bursting it like a plastic bag of cooking blood.

Even holding the shield so tightly above him that he was withdrawn into the protection of the car surrounding him like a tortoise into its shell, there were enough small spaces for the burning napalm to enter to pose a serious problem.

He wasn't exposed enough to be killed outright, but enough flame did get through to cause searing agony as the fire reached his arms, shoulders, and the back of his head.

Phoenix cried out, fighting the instinctive reflex to let go of the shield, knowing that to do so would mean his certain death as a burning human shishkabob, to the delight of the maniacally cheering crowds below.

Another lurch and Phoenix felt the car right itself again.

The heat slowly ebbed from the surface of the shield, and Phoenix could smell the sickening stench of his own charbroiled flesh, feel the pain beginning to cut through beneath the anesthesia of his own adrenalin.

He released the shield and cautiously allowed himself to peak from under it, the tiny trickle of air on his sweaty face feeling like a rush from heaven as the car careened around another steep incline.

Applause!

Catcalls!

"Way to go, Phoenix!" he heard the psychopathic court jester's voice ring out over the public-address system as he shot past the bottom of the run again.

And then Phoenix was shooting helter-skelter up the dizzying incline toward the top of the tracks again, the second car in hot pursuit, autobursts screaming past his ears and making ugly whining sounds as they ricocheted off the sides of the car.

This time would be it. Phoenix knew he would not survive another run through the loop-the-loop.

All it would take would be a bullet fragment to a nonvital area. Not enough to kill or even seriously wound him, but enough to rip muscle tissue to shreds so he would not have the strength to hold the shield over him.

Phoenix took the makeshift sword and began hacking at the chain which held him bolted to the floor of the iron car, risking a bullet in an attempt at freeing his legs.

Concentrating on breaking the chain meant that he could not concentrate on dodging the hailstorm of tumbling death that came from the blistering fire of the car behind him.

Yet there was no other alternative. The risk had to be taken, the chain had to be severed soon, before he rounded the next peak in the tracks.

Managing to cut halfway through one of the links of the chain, Phoenix felt the savage lurch as the car reached the top of the rise.

Grasping the shield with one hand and hooking its edge around the side of the open car to keep it in position, he struggled with the metal sword to cut through the rest of the chain as the car plunged quickly down the steep incline.

Now it shot forward, making a rapid ascent to the top of the Cyclone.

Phoenix was almost through the link.

A black sun exploded in his brain!

A bullet had torn a hunk out of his shoulder the size of a fifty-cent piece. The slug ricocheted around in the car and Phoenix flashed in an instant that it was just a fragment that had passed clean through him. Nevertheless, it had ripped the muscles of his right arm to shreds.

The car suddenly lurched as it sped up toward the crest of the rise. In another second it would be over the top of the track. Phoenix could already see the flamethrower guy shooting a burst of fire through the loop-the-loop and hear the crowd go berserk as they howled for Phoenix to go down in flames.

Blood was pouring fast and hot from the wound in Phoenix's shoulder, covering the seat and puddling the floor of the car.

Phoenix screamed as a second volley drilled a lance of hellfire into his side and catapulted him forward over the edge of the speeding car.

22

Waves of pain and nausea hammered at the doomed man in the runaway roller coaster. His knuckles whitened as his hands gripped the iron roll bar in a viselike grip to prevent him tumbling out onto the tracks.

Stripped of the crash bar which was locked tightly over the legs of passengers when the roller coaster ride had been a harmless amusement, the car was now a treacherously brutal deathtrap. The only thing preventing Phoenix from being catapulted from the car was the firm grip on the iron roll bar running horizontally across the front of the car.

To let go for an instant might mean a grisly death beneath the razor-edged wheels. As he careened helter-skelter around the treacherously canted, curlicueing roller coaster tracks, there was no telling when the car might suddenly lurch to one side and send him hurtling from it, to be dragged beside it by the chain attached to his foot.

Clearing the crest of the hump in the Clone's tracks, the car tipped over the edge and began hurtling to the bottom of the run, gathering velocity as its downward momentum began to increase.

Bounced around inside the madly hurtling crash car like an insect inside a tin can, Phoenix heard his teeth rattle as the vibrations of the wheels bounced his tailbone up and down on the hard metal seat, and heard the wind whistle past his ears and felt its pressure whip back his hair and dig hollows in the flesh of his face.

In a few heartbeats more, the car would slam hard into the concave stretch of track at the bottom of the run and everything would shift into reverse with mind-numbing velocity and bone-crushing force.

Phoenix was a dead man and there was no way to prevent it.

His options were zero. In a few more seconds he'd be slingshot toward the crest of the second hump in the tracks, the highest one with the spotlighted sign across it. After that, he could kiss the shit goodbye.

Next stop would be the loop-the-loop, where the lunatic scuzzbag with the flamethrower was hunkered on a ledge at the center, waiting to hose down the car with a crucifying spray. Phoenix knew in the pit of his gut that this time around the guy wouldn't hold anything back.

He'd be shooting to kill, going at it with a savage vengefulness, pouring on the flame to barbecue Phoenix as his car screamed around the interior of the loop.

Phoenix braced for the bone-crusher impact as the car hit the bottom of the run, feeling the fluttering in his guts he'd used to experience on a fast-moving elevator as the car's trajectory flattened out suddenly, only ten times as hard.

A microsecond later, the car carommed off the turn as the incredible force of its momentum catapulted it up the nearly vertical grade toward the top of the tracks with enough centrifugal force to crush Phoenix back against the seat.

In the few brief seconds left to him before the car screamed over the top and took him on a one-way ride to Napalm City, Phoenix fought the numbness in his mind caused by being whirled around in a savage centifuge for the better part of the last hour.

There were no choices left. No reason to hedge his bets a second longer.

Up ahead, gleaming under the halogen floods on either side, the billboard running across the top of the next hump was supported on two metal poles. There was about four feet of clearance between the head of a rider in the car and the crossbar between the two metal poles which supported the sign.

The clearance had been calculated so that, with the legs of the passengers securely clamped in place by the crash bar of the roller coaster car, no wiseguy would be able to latch onto the sign's crossbar as the car sped beneath it. In order to do that, even a guy with a basketball player's reach would have to stand to a crouch, which there was no way of doing with the crash bar clamping your legs in place.

With the crash bar removed, though, there was now no problem with Phoenix reaching up and grabbing a handhold on the crossbar beneath the floodlit sign.

There would be a major problem, though, in what would happen a split instant after he'd latched onto the crossbar. At that point the wrenching impact of contact would be so powerful that Phoenix had no guarantee that his arms wouldn't be ripped right out of their sockets.

But that wasn't even a serious problem compared to having the chain which held him shackled to the floor of the car ripping off his leg, dismembering him instantly. There'd been enough time for Phoenix to partially sever one of the links of the chain, but there was no telling if he'd weakened it enough for it to snap when the crunch came down.

There was only one way to find out about all of this, though, and only seconds remaining to make his move. If he didn't move his ass fast, he'd be flamebroiled and the matter would be purely academic anyway.

Rising to a half crouch as the car's forward momentum slowed somewhat while it climbed the steep grade, Phoenix turned slightly and flung the shield at the speeding badass crew behind him, simultaneously reaching upward as far as he could for the crossbar on top of the poles holding the sign which marked Clone's highest point.

Phoenix strained to grasp the bar as the car whipped forward. The pain in his fingers was agonizing as they clutched desperately at the metal bar, twisting Phoenix's features into a grotesque mask which mirrored the torment he experienced.

As the car's forward momentum sent it speeding out from beneath him, beginning its final slalom run to the bottom of the speedway before shooting up again into the fiery loop-the-loop, Phoenix molded his hands into an iron vise.

A micro-instant later, the car's velocity jerked against the chain securing his foot with such tremendous force that Phoenix was afraid his leg would be yanked right out of its socket.

Then he felt the pressure's sudden release give as the link of the chain he had succeeded in weakening snapped suddenly, his foot jerked free, and the car plunged down the steep slope of the incline. Lighter by the 200-odd pounds of its passenger's weight, the car now moved at twice its previous speed.

On the follow-through, Phoenix swung his legs up over the bar and tucked them toward his chin as the car carrying the badass murder crew whipped beneath him, the speed of its momentum slinging them past him before they had a chance to draw a bead on him with their weapons, and carrying them at breakneck speed down toward the bottom of the fatal slalom run.

One guy at the back of the car almost got lucky, though. A wild slug ricocheted off the side of the track and a fragment zinged past Phoenix's ear.

Another stray bullet tore a bloody furrow along the muscle tissue of Phoenix's thigh as the badass crew hurtled back up the tracks toward the circle of fire.

Phoenix heard their screams as the kill crew hustled

full-tilt toward the loop-the-loop. One of them had succeeded in jumping from the car before it reached the inferno that awaited it, but the momentum of his jump doomed him before he even left the car.

The badass's sideways inertia carried him over the edge of the roller coaster's tracks and he plummeted over the side, tumbling over and over before crashing into the stands below him.

The car containing the three remaining badasses sped up into the loop of fire.

Burning liquid napalm crashed over them, the flaming jelly sticking to where it touched their bodies. It instantly began eating away at the flesh covering their musculature and skeletons.

The bodies flailed and thrashed as the blood bubbled in their veins and the skin turned to a crisp black covering of sizzling charcoal.

The capacity crowd below screamed in a mad blood frenzy as the car exited the loop-the-loop, resembling a bucket full of live, flaming coals. The figures inside the swooping, fast-sweeping car thrashed in agony as the hellfire consumed them.

Then the car came around the first turn and the barbecued goon guys were whipped from it. They spun end-over-end like enormous flaming T-bones steaks as they were catapulted into the crowd 30 feet below them.

Fighting the agonizing pain in his bleeding arms and legs, Phoenix climbed down the network of crossbeams to the ground as the crowd cheered him on.

A badass clutching an Uzi SMG fired off a burst at the running man. Executing a swift tuck and roll, Phoenix came up under the gun and shattered the hardguy's forearm with a palm smash to the area just below the wrist. Whipping the weapon from the injured cowboy, he fired a burst point-blank into the wounded man's face, blowing his head into the night.

Phoenix ran the gauntlet, toward the Thunder Wheel. Up ahead, through a blood haze, he could see DeLaCour lashing out desperately, his massive foot knocking a badass with a wickedly sharp sickle to the ground, only to be replaced with another and yet another.

"Way to go, Phoenix!" he heard the sadistic dwarf's voice ring out across the fairway. "Let's hear it for a real cham-peen!"

Two hardguys laughed maniacally as they each leveled Ruger .45-caliber automatics at the running man. Phoenix caught the first one in the esophagus with a quickburst from the Uzi he'd taken from the dead cowboy, and whipped around to crash the butt of the SMG across the jawline of the second Ruger pointer.

The second guy went down, flopping around in the slippery pool of blood which pumped nonstop from his dead pard's headless neck stump.

Phoenix was almost at the bottom of the spinning ferris wheel. DeLaCour was half mad as sadistic ghouls harried him like hounds with a cornered fox.

Leaping onto the wheel, Phoenix aimed the Uzi at the chains securing the steel-faced giant to the spinning wheel and blew them apart with his last few rounds of .45-caliber ammo. DeLaCour and Phoenix then jumped to the ground, and Phoenix flung the dry and now useless blaster to the dirt. Surrounded on all sides by kill-crazed badasses, they prepared to go down fighting.

"*Stop!*"

The voice of Abraxas rang out over the public-address system. The angry uglies stopped in their tracks. All heads turned as the caped figure, the iron mask on its face gleaming in the torchlight, strode to the head of the crowd while hundreds of figures parted to allow him through.

Abraxas faced Phoenix and the giant from New Orleans. Faraway capered at the Oz warlord's feet, the bells on his jester's cap and boots jingling with an insane rhythm.

"The Wiz will speak! My master will now decide the fates of the Tin Man and the Cowardly Lion!" Faraway shrieked as he hopped up and down. "Listen to the Wizard's words! Hear his matchless wisdom with your own ears! Feel his unequalled mercy with your own heart! See his—"

Abraxas snatched the microphone from Faraway's hands and glared at the motor-mouthed jester.

"All hear my will," his deeply resonant voice said, ringing out across Blastroland. "I, Abraxas, the Wizard of Oz, decree that—"

A thunderous explosion, then another, then a third, fourth, fifth, and sixth, cut the warlord's pronouncement short as the C-4 charges which Bush Doctor and Raven had ringed the seaward side of the Blastroland amusement park with went off in a series of phased detonations.

Reacting instantly, Phoenix and DeLaCour bowled over the gun-toting leather uglies closest to them. Instinctively they ran in the direction away from the detonations, knowing that Raven and the cabbie were responsible for the diversion.

There! Ahead!

Phoenix could see Raven and Bush Doctor limned in the flickering, strobing light of the detonating charges.

"Let's go!" Phoenix yelled.

"Where?" asked Raven.

"Straight to hell!" he growled, and grabbing up the M16A2 assault weapon which Raven handed him, sprinted off in the direction of the city housing projects.

Toward The Child.

23

A firestorm swept through Blastroland, the crackling flames racing through the park with demonic speed and devouring it like so much dry tinder.

In a matter of minutes, the amusement park was engulfed in a sea of flames as the multiple C-4 detonations created devastating explosions which smashed the rides and booths and sent them collapsing to the ground, feeding the inferno and creating a vortex of flame that licked at the belly of the lunatic night like the tongue of an angry dragon.

Trapped amid the seething havoc of the amusement park, the denizens of Oz scattered in blind panic toward any direction offering the hope of escape, trampling one another in their mindless rush to avoid the flaming destruction erupting everywhere around them.

Driven insane by the belching fury of the hellish fire geysers shooting skyward as the explosions lifted whole sections of ground and blew them skyward with incredible force, many of those who had watched the Phoenix's roller coaster hellride ran straight into the walls of fire between them and safety.

Their screams were lost amid the crackling and moaning of the raging firestorm as their clothes caught fire, burning quickly through to the skin. Human torches were everywhere, the living firebrands thrashing on the ground in vain attempts to smother the flames which were eating them alive, or flailing their arms while they ran dementedly through the furnace of crucifixion.

Safely outside the fiery ring of devastation which marked the perimeter of the blazing amusement park, Phoenix turned for a moment and stared into the heart of the roaring inferno.

Once again, he thought with a mixture of anger and disgust, the baser side of mankind which the awesome destruction of World War Three had brought to the surface had resulted in a little hell on earth, a hell which swept the mad scum beings who had made a fetish of brutality and an art form of pain into a vortex of destruction.

Look at them as they run, he thought. See one with his hands going to a face which has been burned off by fire. See another spread his arms like fiery wings and do a terminal swan dive off the top of the burning ferris wheel.

See others squat like vultures, ripping the weapons and valuables from the still-twitching corpses, only to draw knives and fight to the death among themselves over the grisly spoils.

How many times since he had been condemned to the savage madhouse of the Dark Messiah's nuke-blasted America had Magnus Trench witnessed such twisted scenes of utter depravity?

How many times had he inhaled the putrid odors of burning flesh, seen the bloodlust in the eyes of his fellow man, and known that he faced something which was no longer human, no longer even animal, more like some insect which ripped and tore blindly at every other living thing.

Too fucking many times, Phoenix knew. Too many times for his own brain and heart not to have been touched by the sickening ugliness which had infested every corner of his world like some cancer which destroyed everything that was good or sane and left a foul disease in its wake.

And now he was near the end of another mad run through the gutted slaughterhouse of Nukeworld U.S.A., a run to reunite himself with his wife and his boy. Would they even recognize the man he was now, thought Phoenix, as he turned away from the firestorm?

Maybe even more importantly, would Magnus Trench ever be able to become the man he was—the man who had now become more savage than the savages, more bestial than the beasts in order to survive in the hellworld of the Dark Messiah?

Phoenix and DeLaCour, having regrouped with Raven and Bush Doctor, hightailed it across Surf Avenue toward the city housing project towers which soared like obscene colossi above the hellground below them, stone giants laughing at the puny flesh-and-blood beings which ran like frightened insects through the burning streets of hell.

In the all-consuming chaos, Phoenix and company were just four more figures scurrying through the flames and the rubble in a rush toward cover from the mindbending night.

It wasn't just the explosions of the charges that Raven and Bush Doctor planted that was making the night explode, though.

Forking bolts of lightning speared down from the skies as though the gods themselves were angry, seeking to pass a terrifyingly heavy judgment call on humankind below.

Where lightning struck the ground, the earth shook. Enormous fissures opened in the concrete and asphalt skin of the earth as the bedrock yawned wide like the exposed guts of a corpse on an autopsy table. The quaking ground swallowed scores of the fleeing children of Oz, and they disappeared forever into the sudden chasms in the streets.

Forks of hellfire speared and lanced down from the

clouded underbelly of the sky, crackling over the 60-story towers of the housing projects and surrounding them with a multicolored aurora-borealis effect that made the air crackle with static electricity.

Closer.

Closer.

Closer!

Feeling the ground tremble beneath him and dodging the fissures that were opening as the earthquake rocked the Wizard's domain, Phoenix was moving closer to The Child. He could feel the mutant being's presence within the housing project's central tower, knew that it waited beyond the anonymous brick walls.

Thunder rolled and pealed across the belching, churning heavens. Behind the Phoenix crew, Blastroland was a seething morass of fiery eruptions which spurted and geysered into the pitch black night.

Outlined against it, the dark silhouettes of human figures thrashed and flailed limbs wreathed in hellfire as they raced helter-skelter to escape the violent convulsions of a world gone completely insane.

Hellish shadow beings straight out of a canvas of the Last Judgment by the demented Dutch painter Heironymus Bosch, they were a study in death and destruction.

The presence of The Child was strongest here.

Here.

Where the 60-story building's lower wall had been ruptured by the sudden seismic shock to create a hole two men could easily walk through.

Phoenix looked at the other members of the team for confirmation of what he was about to do. Raven and DeLaCour nodded their agreement. Bush Doctor flashed Phoenix the thumbs-up. Phoenix nodded back in silent gratitude.

Together, they stepped through the hole in the building wall into the smashed lobby.

Inside, The Child had been waiting for them.

Its vast mutant bulk filled the entire building lobby,

taking up at least 30 feet. The body was a huge, translucent blob, its surface covered by a branching network of veins and arteries.

Stunted limbs, like the limbs of thalidomide babies, stuck out of the bloated mass of flesh.

The enormous blob pulsed and quivered as liquids flowed through the network of veins which branched across the surface of its body. Inside the sickeningly translucent flesh, misshapen organs could be seen throbbing rhythmically.

Growing from the sides of The Child were a network of pink, fleshy, rootlike appendages which seemed to anchor the mutant's enormous carcass to the floor and the walls, as though The Child sucked nourishment from the stone and the concrete and the earth itself.

Lightning flickered, and in that brief flash Phoenix could see the face of The Child at one end of the enormous jellylike hulk. Suddenly, the ground shook violently. DeLaCour grabbed Raven, who was almost hurled to the floor. Pieces of plaster and brick fell from the ceiling 20 feet up.

The Child's face was like nothing Phoenix had ever seen. It held him in a mesmeric grasp, as if it were a mirror reflecting his soul like a multifaceted diamond.

It was the face of an angel.

The face of a devil.

The face of utter purity.

The face of foulest corruption.

The head was a shapeless pulpy mass, rounded at the top but tapering to a point so that it resembled an enormous turnip, as though the flesh had rolled itself into a pinkish tube of see-through flesh, and two enormous eyes—as cold and as shiny as polished spheres of black onyx—shone from either side. The face had only a small bud of a mouth and two small slits for nostrils.

A voice spoke inside Phoenix's head as the lunatic night exploded into another deafening thunder peal.

The Child's voice.

As ugly as the mammoth mutant being was, the voice it projected was soft, oddly soothing in tone, caressing the lobes of the brain like a pair of gentle hands, fluttering through the nerve pathways of the brain like a flock of butterflies.

It is pointless, spoke the voice.

Phoenix understood. Pictures went along with the voice. Pictures of an exodus from Liberty Base. Pictures of his wife and son spinning out into the night, taken far from him on board an Apache helicopter which screamed off toward the west with the rising of the sun.

Destroy me, the voice spoke again. *Carry out your mission.*

A jagged bolt of lightning suddenly lit up the interior of the housing project, turning the blackness into daylight for the space of a few split seconds. The ground shook again, more fiercely than before.

"Damn it!" DeLaCour shouted. "The whole fucking place is gonna collapse!"

"My heart's pumping piss!" screamed Bush Doctor. "So I'm gonna split, with your permission."

As the peal of thunder rolled and echoed through the concrete cavern of the building interior, Phoenix realized that another figure was inside the obscene cathedral to the mutant god-thing the denizens of Oz had called The Child.

Lightning split the night again.

Abraxas stood in the strobing violence of the blinding lightning flash, his iron mask gleaming with a mad rhythm as the bolt of energy lit up the cathedral of the damned.

Phoenix raised the M16A2 in his hand and pointed it at Abraxas. But the Wizard of Oz had come prepared.

"Game over," he screamed.

Holding a FRAG grenade in each hand, Abraxas clutched the deadly explosives and with a savage scream sprinted forward toward The Child. The gelatinous membrane of the immense mutant's body made obscene sucking noises as Abraxas passed through it and was absorbed by The Child.

Phoenix and company dodged out the gaping hole in the foundation wall as the explosions detonated within The Child's mammoth jellylike body.

They dove for cover as some diabolical chain reaction made the building collapse behind them as the lightning continued spearing down and tore enormous chunks of brick and concrete from the roof of the building.

A gigantic fissure appeared along one side of the housing project tower. Then another, and then another. The cracks widened as the entire 60-story structure shook and trembled.

Then with a roar that came straight from the throat of hell, the housing project tower burst apart as a searing fireball exploded from its rupturing interior, showering pieces of pulverized rubble over a one-mile radius.

Phoenix and his crew took cover from the jagged concrete hellstorm inside the gutted metal hulk of one of the many derelict city buses littering the housing project's plaza until the death hail subsided.

It was quiet when they emerged, long minutes later.

Strangely, deathly quiet.

The rumblings from within the quaking earth had quieted down like the convulsions of a man whose fever has just broken.

And then, with unexpected suddenness, the night burst into a chorus of screams.

A torch appeared in front of them, and the jester leapt forward, brandishing a burning firebrand clutched in both of his small fists.

Behind the dwarf were scores of the lunatic denizens of the Wizard's realm, watching The Child and its profane father die in a series of explosions.

"The Child has chosen you!" cried the dwarf at Phoenix, pointing the torch toward him. "He has chosen you to lead us."

Then, one by one, more torches appeared in the windswept nightworld of Coney Island, until thousands of the Wizard's profane children stood holding their fires aloft as flame belched through the top of the project's roof, and a hideous scream rode the waves of the dying storm.

"Lead us!" cried the children of Oz.

"Lead us!"

Cries from thousands of throats rivaled, then surpassed the sound of the peals of thunder, building to a crescendo of human voices which echoed crazily across the burning wasteland of Coney Island.

Epilogue

A pounding surf crashed mercilessly against the boulder-strewn shores of Liberty Island, surging with an hypnotic cadence.

DeLaCour, Raven, and Bush Doctor stood beside an ancient stone cannon and allowed the man called Phoenix to be alone with the screaming demons in the private hell he called his mind.

Hours before, the SCORF base at Liberty Island had been alive with activity. The engines of military transport vehicles grunted like prehistoric beasts prowling through primeval swamps while Apache helicopters lifted off into the night, their jet turbines screaming like banshees as they banked and shot away toward the distant horizon.

Chinook and Jolly Green Giant helos had joined the Apaches, their huge steel bellies packed with military vehicles, ordnance, laboratory equipment, and the troops of the Special Commando Retaliatory Force which were the Dark Messiah's elite.

Inside the lead helo, guarded by a heavily armed contingent of SCORF troopers, John Tallon smiled sardonically as he watched the nuke-blasted city spiraling away from him. It was the smile of a soldier whose mission had been accomplished.

Hours before, the Dark Messiah and the wife and son

of Magnus Trench, the man who was called Phoenix, had been spirited off toward underground bases near the Chicago Urban Containment Zone.

Somebody had once said that the child was father to the man. The techs wouldn't give guarantees, but the son of Magnus Trench might be as good a donor of Immune antibodies as his father.

Below the heliborne airlift convoy, Liberty Island erupted into a burning maelstrom as the phased charges planted by demolition men blew the hardbase to hell and gone.

The dynamited accessways to the underground hardbase would seal the Liberty Base complex off beneath tons of wreckage until SCORF was ready to occupy it again.

Whatever vehicles could not be airlifted off the island were driven over the concrete ramparts of the island and into the sea.

The half-submerged hulks of the trashed military vehicles bobbed in the pounding surf of the powerful currents at the mouth of Upper New York Bay . . . .

Liberty Island was as deserted as the surface of the moon when Phoenix and the others had arrived there.

Now Phoenix stood on the windswept island beneath the 600-foot statue of a woman in a nightgown covered with filth. He looked out across the glittering obsidian black surface of the water.

Flames danced on Manhattan Island. Bizarre lights flickered at the topmost reaches of the scorched and flashmelted steel skeletons of the skyscrapers, like candles placed behind the empty eye sockets of so many skulls.

The night was filled with fire as thousands of torches were held aloft in the wreckage of the streets, moving like a stream of liquid lava through the mass graveyard of the gutted urban hellzone.

Before daylight dawned on Nuked York City, corpses would be piled waist-deep amid the shattered concrete rubble of the raped metropolis's streets.

A firestorm was coming. The scum denizens of the nightmare they called Oz were on the warpath tonight. Badass troops were massing by the thousands along the tip of Lower Manhattan. Preparing for an assault on the Dark Messiah's loony-toon city of Luxor.

Fires still burned in places, flames shooting and spurting from the wreckage and gushing up from the craters in the concrete plaza surrounding the Statue where the TNT charges had ruptured power lines and gas mains.

A pall of noxious smoke from the burning wreckage of the SCORF hardbase hung over the island in a putrid cloud which slowly drifted across the East River. The smoke rose high into the air, obscuring the enormous statue's body.

Phoenix trudged through the cinders of Liberty Island, toward the base of the abandoned colossus. He mounted the low stone steps which brought him through the arched entranceway into Lady Liberty's base, walking past huge iron doors which hung uselessly from their massive dynamited hinges.

Booted feet crunched across rubble and broken glass and echoed off the narrow iron stairs which spiraled up like some colossal spinal column of black wrought iron to a height of 30 stories, ending in the crowned head of Lady Liberty.

Phoenix took the iron spirals of Lady Liberty's iron spine at a full run, challenging his pumping legs to propel his body up the grueling, dizzying ascent to the Statue's mammoth metal head, feeling the sweat pour from his body to form a glistening film on his face and limbs, and hearing his heart beat like a jackhammer as he hustled to the top of the run.

Tallon had used him. To bring Abraxas down. To neutralize the warlord's growing threat to the Dark Messiah's forces. Expecting the bloodbath to follow but not caring. Content to return when the tribes of the city had become weakened without Abraxas to guide them.

The Dark Messiah was a patient man. He had all the time in the world.

Tallon had put his enemy inside a box after all. In possession of the only thing Magnus Trench gave a damn about in the hellblasted world, the Dark Messiah's merc enforcer had clipped the wings of the Phoenix.

He had now succeeded where he had failed before. Phoenix would come to him. And this time he would wait. Wait and plan. The diseased bodies of the woman and child would be kept on continuous life support as long as they were needed.

In the end, they would watch their father die. Slowly. Horribly. And there would be nothing any power on earth could do to prevent it.

Tallon would only have to wait.

Wait and plan.

Faster, harder! Phoenix had barely scaled the statue's first ten stories. He had to reach the top. Let his heart burst before he made it, he didn't give a damn.

They had taken them. Sandra and Brian. Where, he didn't know. Why he could not say. Yet somewhere Phoenix was certain his wife and son were still alive. He felt the knowledge in his gut.

Tallon would not abandon his single hold over Magnus Trench. The merc honcho never destroyed what he could profit by. He hated them, yes. But he would not kill them. Not yet.

Phoenix was almost at the top of the run.

His legs felt as though they were sacks of lead. His chest was on fire as his lungs strained to suck enough oxygen out of the air to feed the starving heart and supply energy to the heavily overtaxed muscles.

Phoenix took the final spiral and staggered toward the shadowy doorway giving access into the monstrous steel head of the mammoth statue.

Now having reached the top, Phoenix could see the light of the full moon spilling into the immense windows in the Lady's spike-bristling crown, casting planes of silvery brilliance through the two enormous eyes.

He took the last spiraling flight of stairs two at a time, collapsing on the filthy floor that was strewn with a jumble of human skeletons that had been sightseers on the terrible day the nukes had exploded.

Phoenix picked himself up and looked out the windows in the Lady's head. He saw the city radiating outward in every direction, a nightmare world where the Wizard's badass minions were massing against the Dark Messiah's children of chaos.

"Wiz?"

It was Abraxas's dwarf. How long he had been staring, lost in his own thoughts, Phoenix didn't know. He hadn't even heard the jingling of the bells which hung from the jester's costume.

"Go away."

"I won't," returned the jester. "You've been chosen. You're our new Wizard." A perverted smile crossed the dwarf's cadaverous face and a malicious light twinkled in his beady black pushbutton eyes.

"They're waiting for you to give the word," said Faraway. "What's the good word, Wiz? Is it 'blood?' Is it 'death?' Is it 'fire?' How about 'tally-ho?' That's always a good one, isn't it?"

Phoenix smiled a jagged smile that was more like a grimace. The badasses of Oz were ready to scream down on Luxor, the Dark Messiah's perverse city of light in the center of microwaved Manhattan Island. It was a confrontation that had to happen sooner or later with SCORF out of the picture and Abraxas a bittersweet memory to his children of chaos.

It wasn't Phoenix's fight. It meant nothing to him. By the time the battle was over he would be far from Nuked York City.

Where, he didn't care.

How, he didn't know.

Why, he couldn't say.

"You do the honors, little man," Phoenix said, turning away from one of the observation windows in

Lady Liberty's vast iron head. "I've had enough killing for one season in hell."

Phoenix handed the Very pistol to Faraway, watching the midget's eyes light up with demented glee as he grasped the gun's grip in both tiny hands and, leaping onto the window ledge, aimed it at the sky and fired a red flare high into the churning black cauldron of the psychotic night.

"Wiz?" Faraway asked, turning from the window. "Wiz, you gotta come back! Your faithful army needs you for inspiration . . . Wiz, Wiz—"

But Phoenix was already lost in the shadows of the colossus, his boots clanging dully on the spiraling metal stairs as he hustled to the ground, a shadow in the belly of a shadow, with a mad fool in its empty head, moving painfully toward his own final end, knowing that sometimes pain was the only thing a man had to let him know he was alive.